KILLED AT HOME

Readers are encouraged to go to www.MissionPointPress.com to contact the author or to find information on how to buy this book in bulk at a discounted rate.

Published by Mission Point Press
2554 Chandler Lake Rd.
Traverse City, MI 49686
(231) 421-9513
www.MissionPointPress.com

ISBN: 978-1-943995-41-7
LOC: 2017912749

Printed in the United States of America.

This is a work of fiction. Names, places, and incidents are the products of the author's imagination or are used fictitiously. Any resemblance to actual events or locales or persons, living or dead, is entirely coincidental.

KILLED AT HOME

A MYSTERY BY
STUART SAFFT

MISSION POINT PRESS

Chapter 1

"**J**oe. Ginny. In here. Now!"

As the chief bellowed these words from his doorway, everyone in the Jasper Creek Police Department's large, open room turned and silently looked at Joe McFarland and Ginny Harris, wondering what kind of trouble Joe had gotten himself and his partner into this time.

Joe and Ginny immediately dropped what they were working on and briskly marched into the chief's office.

"Chief, whatever it was that we did this time, it was all me. Ginny wasn't involved," said Joe as he closed the chief's door.

"No, Chief. That's not tr—," said Ginny before she was cut off by the chief.

"Miracles of miracles. I didn't call you two in here to bawl you out. This time. But we do have a problem."

"What is it?" asked Ginny.

The chief sat down behind his gray, metal desk. Joe and Ginny followed suit, sitting in the two small visitor chairs in front of the desk.

"Carl Wallerman was just found dead in his home."

"Who's Carl Wallerman?" asked Joe.

"One of our town councilmen," said Ginny. "You've lived here long enough to know these things already."

"Well, I know who our mayor is, and our prosecutor. And, of course," nodding toward the chief, "our police chief. I think that's all I need to know about local politics to do my job."

"Joe, you also need to be more informed and involved as a local citizen."

"Yeah. I'll be sure to add that to my already-overflowing bucket list."

The chief slammed the side of his fist on his cluttered desk. "All right, children. Can you hold your civics discussion until you're on your own time?"

"Uh, yes, of course. Sorry, Chief," said Ginny.

"Back to our problem. Wallerman's been a member of the Council for the past five or six years. And the mayor, the other council members and everyone else, plus their brothers and sisters, are going to want this, which sure looks like something other than a natural death, solved yesterday."

"And I guess you're handing the case to us," said Joe.

"No, I invited you in here for milk and cookies. Damn right I'm handing this case to you. And I want it solved. Quickly. This is now far and away your top priority. And your second and third priorities as well."

"Gotcha."

"Chief, what else can you tell us?" asked Ginny.

"Not much. He was found in his study at home by his cleaning woman when she arrived a little while ago. She called 9-1-1. He was already cold by the time the medics got there."

"OK, we're on it. How long ago did we get the call?" asked Ginny.

"About 20 minutes. Officer Segura radioed it in almost

immediately after he arrived there in response to the 9-1-1 call."

"Chief, we're on our way."

"Let's see if we can wrap this up fast and sweet."

"We'll do our best," said Ginny.

On their way out, Joe and Ginny stopped at Dispatch to listen to the cleaning woman's call to 9-1-1, get the address of Wallerman's house and listen to Officer Segura's radio message.

Chapter 2

Ten minutes later, Joe pulled out of the parking lot and abruptly cut into traffic. Sitting in the passenger seat, Ginny decided not to say anything about Joe's driving, allowing a few minutes for Joe to cool down from their meeting with the chief.

Joe broke the silence a few minutes later. "Ginny, whaddaya know about this Wallerman?"

"Not much. I voted for him last time, but only because he was an incumbent and I figured that might make him more effective than a newbie."

"Hate to show my bias, but I wish we just had a mayor without a town council sitting on top of him."

"Why?"

"It's harder to get anything decided. Take our pay raises. Not surprisingly, the chief has to make a proposal to the mayor. But the mayor can't decide. He reviews it, adds his comments to the chief's proposal and then sends it to the town council for their approval. Or rejection. Or, as is usually the case, approval of a whittled down increase."

"Joe, my understanding is that many towns and smaller cities have both a mayor and a town council."

"Fine. But that doesn't make it right. I think it's just duplicate BS and bureaucracy. And decisions by a committee, even if it's comprised of well-meaning volunteers, are never as straightforward as decisions by one person in charge."

"Well, in any event, Joe, it is what it is. One question for us is whether or not Wallerman's homicide had anything to do with his town council work."

"Can't argue with that."

Fifteen minutes later, Joe pulled up behind two patrol cars parked in front of Wallerman's house. Joe wasn't surprised to see the coroner's and the crime scene investigators' vans parked in the driveway. Nor was he surprised, given the neighborhood, about the house: large, two stories, a long driveway going around the right side of the house, presumably to a garage. The entire structure was white-painted brick, with light-gray shutters at every window. The large lawn was immaculately cared for, with a row of short, red azalea bushes running along the entire length of the house. The front door was open, with a uniformed patrolman standing directly in front of it.

Joe and Ginny got out of the car and walked up.

"Morning, Officer," said Ginny as she and Joe flashed their badges.

"Morning, Detectives. They're all inside. The study where they found him is off to the left."

"Thanks," said Joe. "Where's Segura?"

"In there someplace. Last I knew he was in the kitchen. Straight back on the right."

Joe and Ginny walked into the house. Without a word or signal to each other, they both headed straight back to the kitchen. Sure enough, Patrolman Segura was sitting at the center island with a large mug of coffee in front of him.

"Morning, Officer. I'm Detective Harris and this is Detective McFarland. Got a few minutes?"

"Looks like I've got all the time in the world. The sarge told me to just sit here in the kitchen."

"We've got a few questions to help us get up to speed," said Joe. "But first, any more of that coffee? It smells great."

"Yeah. And it is good coffee. There's an almost full pot over there," the officer replied, pointing to the pot and mugs on the counter next to the refrigerator. "Help yourself."

"Great. Hold on while we grab some," said Joe.

Joe filled two large mugs and took a sip from one, thinking how he hadn't expected to be drinking a dead man's coffee this morning — but it was damn good.

As Joe walked back to Ginny, coffees in both his big hands, Ginny found herself surprised by how impressed she still was by his size, even after several nights in his bed. At six-foot-four, he wasn't the largest officer in the department, but he was solid. Even though she wasn't a football fan, she knew enough to give him fullback status. When he handed her the cup of coffee, she could see the bulge of his forearm through his shirt and suit jacket.

Turning to Segura as she took a sip, Ginny asked, "Officer, why don't you walk us through what happened?"

"Will do. At 8:37, Dispatch sent me here in response to a 9-1-1 call. Got here 8:45 on the nose. Turns out the 9-1-1 call was from the vic's housekeeper, a Donata Milani. She'd just arrived to clean the house and saw the body when she walked in. She quickly concluded he was dead and called 9-1-1."

"Did she check his pulse? Or try CPR?" asked Joe.

"No. She told me she could just tell he was dead. Said she doesn't know how to do CPR."

"OK. Then what?"

"I radioed this in, indicating it was a homicide. Corpses don't dispose of the gun after they kill themselves. Twenty minutes later, the usual crowd started arriving. As soon as the sarge got here, he told me to come and stay here in the kitchen. And that's what I been doing."

"I take it you didn't see anything unusual when you got here," said Ginny.

"That's correct. Nothing. Other than the body, of course."

"OK, thanks, Officer. We're heading for the study to talk with some of the others. We may have more questions later," said Joe.

"Sure 'nuff."

Joe and Ginny walked back toward the front of the house and entered the study. Ginny wasn't even sure they'd fit into the small room. Crammed in were the coroner and two of his assistants, three crime scene investigators, the sergeant and the county prosecutor. Not to mention the dead victim. And now the two detectives.

Looking at the victim, Ginny couldn't help noting how comfortable he appeared. Sitting in his plush leather desk chair, with his left arm dangling over the side and his head leaning on his left shoulder, he seemed to be peacefully asleep. Except, of course, for the bullet hole in the center of his forehead, and the front of his light blue robe covered in blood. Wallerman looked to be in his mid-50s. He had a full head of hair, dark brown except for graying sideburns. He appeared to be trim and well built. It was difficult to judge his height while he was slouched in his chair.

"Good morning, all," said Ginny as she and Joe gave half-hearted waves to everyone.

Most everyone grunted or nodded in response.

Joe and Ginny walked over toward the body.

The coroner said, "Good morning, Detectives."

"Morning, Doc. Whaddaya have?" asked Ginny. Joe merely nodded.

"Two well-placed shots, one to the head and one to the chest. Hard to tell which was the kill shot. Either would have done the job nicely. Looks like the shooter knew what he, or she, was doing. Both shots were through and through."

Ginny stared at the wall where the chest bullet had already been dug out of the godawful splash of red on the drywall.

The coroner pointed to the window molding behind the desk. "It was easy to get the one bullet out of the drywall. But the forensic guys had to cut out the section of molding because the other bullet was buried in it. The bullet that was in the drywall is damaged pretty badly, but it looks to be a 10mm. We'll know more once we get both bullets back to the lab."

"Estimated TOD?" asked Joe.

"Again, we'll know more later, but I'd estimate sometime between eight and midnight last night. But this is all preliminary. Given the high profile of the vic, I've called in the state investigators. They're a couple of hours out. Wrapping up a scene on the other side of Columbus."

"I don't think we'll hang around waiting for the BCI guys," said Joe.

Joe and Ginny handed the coroner their cards and Ginny said, "Please give them these and ask them to contact us if they learn anything more or different than what you've told us."

"Will do."

"OK, thanks," said Ginny.

Joe and Ginny then turned to County Prosecutor Charles Porter, who was talking with one of the crime scene techs.

"Hi, Charles," said Ginny. "This must be a big one to get you, rather than one of your APAs, at the crime scene."

"Hi, Ginny. Joe. Yeah, this is a big one. Someone killing a town council member is not an everyday event. Not even an every week or every month event. And especially with Carl's history."

"History? Fill us in. We just caught this one and haven't had any time to start checking into things."

"Well, way back when, Carl was actually an assistant prosecuting attorney in our office. It was before my time, but I've heard good things about his work."

"So I take it he left the prosecutor's office at some point."

"About 15 years ago. He went over to the other side."

"Another one who became a defense attorney?" asked Joe.

"You got it. Guess he finally decided he might as well get paid a living wage for the work he was doing."

"That's just great," said Joe.

"What do you mean?" asked Porter.

"We've been here less than 30 minutes," said Joe. "And

we've already got hundreds of possible suspects." Joe extended an additional finger with each sentence. "Every criminal he prosecuted when he was an APA. Then every defendant he failed to get off. And for every one he did get off, the victim of that defendant. And add in the family and friends of all the above. Man, we'll need a three-ring binder just to hold the names of all the possible suspects."

"I'm sure you guys'll use your bag of tricks to quickly cull the list down to a manageable size."

"We will," said Ginny. "But we also have to look at all the other possible motives unrelated to his legal work." Mimicking Joe's gesture, Ginny extended one of her fingers with each possible motive. "A problem with his town council activities? Or with a coworker? Or a neighbor? Or a former girlfriend? Or the boyfriend of his mistress? Or who knows what?"

"Well, the main thing is that we get his killer soon. The town's powers that be will soon be all over me."

"OK, *thank you*, Charles. Now we know what makes this case so important. Not that a man has been killed, but that you'll be feeling some pressure. In that vein, we're off to talk with the housekeeper who found Wallerman," said Joe.

As they walked away, Ginny leaned close to Joe, stood on her toes and whispered, "Joe, you didn't have to be so sarcastic with Porter."

"Why not? He's a good guy, but he can be a pompous ass sometimes. The main reason to solve this quickly is the pressure that will be on him. Gimme a break. But, not to worry. He's too thick-headed to even have recognized I was being sarcastic."

"OK. Fine."

"Hey, were you being sarcastic with that?" asked Joe with a smile.

"That's for me to know and you to wonder about."

As Ginny straightened back up, Joe again thought to himself how short Ginny was and what an unusual looking couple they must be when they walked side-by-side. But Joe had seen many examples, both in the gym and out on the street, where her short stature belied her wiry strength, agility and speed.

Joe and Ginny walked out of the study and down the hall. There in the living room was a middle-aged woman clearly dressed for doing housecleaning rather than waiting for tea to be served. She was sitting on the edge of one of the two large couches, looking down at her feet. Joe and Ginny walked over to her.

"Excuse me. Ms. Milani?" said Ginny.

"Si, Si. Er, sorry. Yes, I am Donata Milani."

"Ms. Milani," said Ginny. "I'm Detective Harris and this is Detective McFarland. May we ask you a few questions?"

"Yes, yes, of course. Although this won't be of any help to poor Mr. Wallerman."

"No, but it will help us identify his killer. Ms. Milani, what time did you arrive here today?"

"Same as every week. I come every Tuesday. I take the bus and get off at 6th Street. Then I walk here. I always get here a little before 8:30."

"Tell us what happened this morning," encouraged Ginny.

"Like all the times, I use my key to open the front

door. I work for Mr. Wallerman more than four years. He trusts me. He give me a key almost four years ago. So I can come and clean even if he is out of town or just out doing errands. Anyhow, I see through the window that the study light is on, so I go to the study to say good morning. And, my God, I see Mr. Wallerman sitting there. Dead."

"How did you know he was dead?" asked Joe. "Did you check his pulse?"

"No, no. I could not touch him. But I look carefully and see that he is not breathing."

"So then what did you do?" asked Joe.

"I go to the kitchen and call 9-1-1."

"Why not use the phone on Mr. Wallerman's desk in the study?"

"I'm not that dumb. I watch a lot of shows on TV. I know there could be evidence and not to touch it. Stuff like fingerprints. Or DNI."

"You mean DNA."

"Yes, yes. DNA."

"Are you sure the front door was locked when you arrived here?"

"Yes. I remember the clicking sound when I use my key."

"Did you notice anything unusual?" asked Ginny.

"What? Of course! Mr. Waller—"

"I mean other than finding Mr. Wallerman," interrupted Ginny.

"No. Everything else was normal."

"Ms. Milani, we'd appreciate it if you would carefully check the whole house to see if anything looks out of place or is missing. If you see anything, please give me a call. Here's my card."

"OK. So you think you will catch the killer?"

"We think so. We will surely be trying very hard. Thank you for your help."

"Prego. Uh, you are welcome."

Joe and Ginny spent the next few minutes with the crime scene lead investigator.

"There was no jimmying of any doors or windows. We collected several fingerprints, but need time to try and identify whose they are. Doesn't seem to be a robbery gone bad. His wallet and cash are on the dresser in his bedroom, and nothing seems to be disturbed. We're checking any messages on his home phone, and we're taking his cellphone and PC back to the lab. We'll also check his phone and PC at his law offices. We should be able to check everything, but if we need help we'll call in the state guys."

"Sounds good. Let us know what you find," said Joe.

"Will do."

Then the patrol sergeant confirmed to Joe and Ginny that he had officers going door-to-door in a four-block radius. "So far, no one saw or heard anything. But the officers will need to come back this evening to catch those who've already left for work."

"Thanks, Sarge. Let us know if your guys turn up anything," said Joe.

"For sure."

"Joe, I think that's about all we can do here for now. What say we head back and get to work?"

"Get to work? Whaddaya think we've been doing here,

attending a party? But, yeah, you're right. Let's head on back."

As they walked out the front door, Joe said, "Oh, look. Surprise. The vultures are already circling." Joe swept his arm from right to left, indicating the five or six reporters and three cameramen already grouping in the street in front of the house.

"Joe, I know you hate these folks, but give 'em a break. They're just doing their job."

"Yeah, I know, but . . ."

"Let me handle them. Just stay silently at my side."

"With pleasure."

As Joe and Ginny started down the walkway, the reporters and cameramen surged forward, forming a semi-circle directly in Joe and Ginny's path.

"Detectives, what can you tell us?"

"Detectives, do you know who . . .?"

"Why do you think . . .?"

"Hold on. Hold on," said Ginny. "We've just started the investigation. We've got nothing to say at this point. I'm sure you'll hear from the PD or the prosecutor's office when there's something to report. Now, if you'll please excuse us."

Squeezing and pushing through the crowd and looking carefully at the growing group of neighbors standing in the street staring at the house, Joe and Ginny reached Joe's car. They were quickly buckled in and on their way back to the station.

Chapter 3

"**O**K," said Ginny, as she and Joe carried coffees to their back-to-back desks and sat down. "Time to start digging."

"Definitely," said Joe. "Cuz we have to stop soon for lunch."

"No argument there. But let's tackle the vic first. What say I try to gather some background from the Internet while you check our files and DMV? Then after lunch, we can go around the corner and see what we can learn at the town council's and mayor's offices."

"Can't argue with that."

About an hour later, Joe said, "OK. Let's see what we've learned and then head to lunch."

"Works for me. You first?"

"Sure. Mine's easy. I didn't learn squat. He's got an Ohio driver's license. One speeding ticket three years ago. No rap sheet. Nothing in the state or FBI files and no military service. Looks like he was either a plain, boring person or a very successful, well-camouflaged super spy."

"Not sure if it's anything useful, but I've got a few more facts from the Internet."

"OK, shoot."

"He was 52 when he was killed. Born in Pittsburgh, but his family moved to Cleveland when he was five. After high school in Cleveland, he went to Ohio State at their main campus in Columbus. Majored in psychology.

Law school at the University of Dayton. He worked for a small law firm in Dayton for four years and then joined the prosecutor's office here as an assistant prosecuting attorney, where he stayed for five years."

"Is that when he moved here?" asked Joe.

"Yes. He initially rented an apartment downtown. After he got married — to wife number one — he bought a small house. And then the large house we were at today with wife number two."

"How many wives in total?" asked Joe.

"Just two. But I'll get to that. Let me continue with where I was."

"OK. Sorry."

"After his five years as an assistant prosecuting attorney, he 'went over to the other side,' as our county prosecutor put it. With Dewey, Cavanaugh and Williams. Then after six years he left and opened his own practice. Best I can tell, other than a combination paralegal and secretary, it's a one-man show. His office is only a few blocks from here on Meredith."

"Given the neighborhood he lives in, and his house, he must have been a pretty successful lawyer. And obviously earning a lot more than he ever did as an APA."

"For sure. In addition, about five years ago, he ran for and was elected to the town council."

"OK. Now give me the juicy part about his two wives."

"Sorry to disappoint you, but nothing too juicy. He was married to his first wife while he was an APA. They got divorced after four years. Incompatibility. No kids."

"How boring."

"He stayed single for 10 years before marrying wife

number two. He managed to stay married to this one for six years. Again, no kids. He's been single ever since."

"Wow. Living in that large house all by himself. I could have sold my tiny place and moved in with him."

"Well, that's about all I've got so far. There are a lot of newspaper articles about him or with his name in the article, but I think we need lunch first."

"Amen to that. Let's cut right to the chase and agree on Sancho's."

"Deal."

Ten minutes later, Joe and Ginny were sitting at their usual table at Sancho's Taco Shop, around the corner from the PD. This was their nearly exclusive lunch place whenever they were at the station when lunchtime rolled around. They finished a bowl of tortilla chips and salsa while waiting for their burritos and Diet Cokes.

"We've got a lot of work to do on this one, Joe."

"No kidding. We need to check criminals he prosecuted, probably focusing on those who he put away and just got out of prison recently. Plus, once he left the prosecutor's office, defendants he unsuccessfully defended and victims of defendants he successfully defended."

"Yup. Not to mention if it's anything with his town council work."

"And then there's his personal life, including wives one and two. Yeah, we'll be busy for a while."

"Yes, we will. Anyway, Joe, here comes our food. Let's enjoy it, after which we'll head over to town hall."

"Good idea, Ginny. Bon appetit, or whatever the Spanish equivalent of that is."

"I think it's *buen provecho*. Anyway, same to you."

After finishing their meals and while waiting for the bill, Ginny asked, "Are we still on for tonight?"

"You bet. A deal is a deal. If you're OK with it, I'll just order a pizza instead of us cooking. That'll give us more time to talk."

"Sounds like a plan, Partner. Now let's pay and get back to work."

Chapter 4

"I'm glad it's only a short walk."

"Getting lazy in your old age?" asked Joe.

"No. It's just that, even if we get to see the mayor, we're unlikely to find the council chairman there. Let's remember that this is a part-time volunteer job for the people on the council."

"Yeah. You're right."

Five minutes later, Joe and Ginny were in the town hall. Up one flight of stairs, and the mayor's office was on their right.

"Good afternoon," said Ginny to the middle-aged, slightly overweight receptionist sitting in a small room outside the mayor's office.

"Good afternoon. How may I help you?"

"We'd like to speak with the mayor. I'm Detective Harris and this is Detective McFarland."

"Oh, my God. Is something wrong?"

"We just want to talk with Mayor Bell about Mr. Wallerman's death."

"Oh. How very sad. Who would want to kill that nice man? Mayor Bell is still at lunch, but should be back in a half hour or so."

"OK. We'll swing by the town council offices. We'll be back a little later."

"Fine. I'll tell the mayor when he returns. I assume you know where the council's offices are."

"Yes, we do. Thanks," replied Ginny as she and Joe turned around and walked back into the hallway and made a left.

Almost all the way down the hall on the left was a door marked "Town Council." Joe and Ginny entered and walked up to another woman, who could have been a twin to the woman they had just left in the mayor's office.

"Good afternoon. We'd like to speak with the town council chairman. We're detectives with the Jasper Creek PD."

"I'm sorry. Mr. Forrester isn't here. As you probably know, being on the town council is a part-time position. Mr. Forrester is a vice president over at First National Bank. I assume you can find him there."

"Could you do us a favor and call to see if we can talk with him for a few minutes if we go over there now? It's about Mr. Wallerman's death."

"That's what I figured. Poor Mr. Wallerman. At least he wasn't currently married and has no children. I'll call Mr. Forrester now."

She called and had a brief discussion. "Yes, Detectives. He'd be happy to speak with you. He'll be expecting you in a few minutes."

"Thank you."

After a 10-minute walk, Joe and Ginny entered the bank, announced themselves to one of the tellers and were immediately ushered into Mr. Forrester's office.

After introductions, Joe and Ginny declined an offer of coffee and sat in two large, comfortable, brown leather chairs in front of the large mahogany desk. Forrester sat in his desk chair on the other side of his desk.

"Thank you for seeing us."

"Don't mention it. Betsy said you wanted to talk about poor Carl. What a shame. How can I help you?"

"Was he having any problems with anyone on the town council?" asked Joe.

"No, not at all. He was well-liked and got along with everyone. I mean, we were often arguing about various town-related things, but it never got personal with anyone."

"How about other government employees?"

"No problems that I'm aware of."

"Are you aware of any problems in his personal life? Was he acting at all strange or did he seem worried recently?"

"Again, nothing that I was aware of. But we didn't really socialize. We rarely saw each other or spoke if it wasn't town council-related."

"Anything unusual about his town council work?"

"No, nothing jumps to mind. Things were pretty much straightforward and noncontroversial."

"What do you mean by 'pretty much?'" asked Ginny.

"Well, it was just that sanctuary stuff. But I can't believe that had anything to do with his death."

"Exactly what sanctuary stuff?" asked Joe.

"You know how some of the major U.S. cities are establishing themselves as so-called sanctuary cities. Where illegal immigrants, or undocumented immigrants if you prefer, can live in reasonable peace and safety. Where the city won't enforce the federal immigration laws or even tell the federal authorities about an illegal who's not doing anything seriously wrong. And where the immigrant can often get access to medical care, in-state college tuition rates, a photo ID and so on."

"Yes, we're well aware of that," said Joe.

"Well. Carl was pushing for and getting ready to officially propose that Jasper Creek become a 'sanctuary town,' if you like. So far, other than one other council member, he didn't have any real support from other council members, but he wasn't giving up. It's unlikely that his proposal would have passed, but now I guess we'll never know."

"Who's the other council member who supported this?"

"That'd be Liz. Elizabeth Gould. She's the one die-hard liberal on the council. She never met a government program or an oppressed group that she didn't love."

"We'll plan on speaking with her. Who knew about this whole sanctuary thing?" asked Ginny.

"The council members, of course. And many others. Neither Carl nor Liz had made any big public statement about it, but they sure weren't keeping it a secret either."

"Do you think someone could have been against this enough to kill Mr. Wallerman because of it?" asked Joe.

"Well. I would have said no. But the way things are going these days . . . Who knows?"

"Any very unhappy constituents?"

"Well, sure. You never have everyone happy about everything we do. Whatever we do, or don't do, you can be sure that someone will be unhappy."

"And threatening letters?" asked Ginny.

"Yes, we get some. But we don't, at least until now, take them seriously."

"Can we see those letters?"

"Betsy at the town council offices keeps any that are addressed to the council or to me. Those that are addressed to other specific council members are given to them unopened. Technically, we can't open mail addressed to another individual."

"Can we borrow those letters that Betsy has?" asked Ginny.

"Sure. I don't see why not. I'll call her to tell her it's OK to give them to you. I'll ask her to type up a receipt for you to sign. No offense, just for our records."

"No problem. Tell Betsy we'll swing by shortly."

"Will do."

"Anything else, Mr. Forrester?"

"No, I don't think so."

"Well, here's my card just in case," said Ginny. "And we may be back if we have additional questions."

"That'll be fine. Sure hope you find the you-know-what who killed him."

"You can be sure that's what we're focused on," said Joe.

The two detectives left the bank and returned to the mayor's office. They had a brief but not useful discussion with the mayor. He knew about Wallerman's desire and efforts to have Jasper Creek become a sanctuary town, but added nothing to what Joe and Ginny had already learned.

They then went back to the town council's offices. Betsy had put all the letters from the past two years into four large envelopes. She also handed Ginny a receipt for these letters, which Ginny signed and gave back to her. When Betsy learned that the detectives were planning to visit Wallerman's law office, she gave them the few pieces of mail that were in Wallerman's mailbox cubbyhole next to her desk. Joe and Ginny weren't going to open these since they didn't have a warrant. Just in case there was something useful to the investigation in these pieces of mail, they would have Wallerman's assistant open them.

Each carrying two of the envelopes, and Ginny carrying the few letters addressed to Wallerman by name, Joe and Ginny left the building and headed for PD headquarters.

Chapter 5

Back at the station, each with a cup of stale coffee, Joe and Ginny settled into the conference room. They were in their regular positions: Joe in one of the chairs, leaning it back on its rear two legs with one of his feet on the table in front of him, and Ginny standing in front of the whiteboard, marker in hand.

"OK, Joe. With so many different avenues to pursue, we better get them all listed and then prioritized."

"Agreed. Here goes. Starting chronologically, with his days in the prosecutor's office. There are the defendants and their family and friends who he put away. And the victims, and their family and friends, of defendants who he failed to put way."

After writing each of these categories on the whiteboard, Ginny continued, "And then there're his years as a defense attorney. Those, along with their family and friends, who he unsuccessfully defended, and the victims, with their family and friends, of defendants he did get off."

"Yup, and let's not forget that sanctuary stuff with the town council. Could be a hate crime if the perp hates immigrants or foreigners. Maybe a hate-crime once removed. They killed the councilman, not one of the immigrants or foreigners. Or it could be someone who didn't want to have a lot of people, regardless of their race or religion, move to Jasper Creek and make everything crowded. Or—"

"Hold on, Joe. Let me get all this on the board.

"OK, got it. Could also be some other town-council issue. And I bet you were going to add all the personal possibilities unrelated to his legal or council work."

"Yeah. It could be anyone from ex-wives to current and ex-girlfriends. Or a neighbor he had a fight with. Maybe even the guy he accidently cut off driving home the other evening. Hell, for all we know, he could have been in the middle of a drug deal gone bad."

"I know. I know. The possibilities are endless. We need to dive in and start shrinking the massive potential-suspect pool." Joe ran his fingers through his hair, gave a heavy sigh, and added, "So, OK, let's start with his assistant prosecuting attorney role and his early defense attorney job. If something here was the motive, Wallerman woulda been killed long ago. Unless the perp wasn't around for several years."

"Yeah, like having been in prison and only recently released."

"My thinking exactly. Let's see if we can get our friendly county prosecutor to have some of his staff research these possibilities for us."

"And then we need to visit the law firm he used to work for and his own law firm to dig through the defendant-side of our multiple possibilities."

"Jeez, Ginny, we'll need a few lucky breaks to whittle this down to a manageable size. But, for now, let's call it a day. I don't even want to start right now on the town council mail we got from Betsy. Time to go home and call the pizza guy."

"OK. Just let me copy down what we have on the board. We need to go in separate cars anyhow. Tomorrow morning I want to stop at the library to see what the newspapers had to say about the vic over the years."

"OK. I'll leave my car in the street and the garage door open. You can pull right in. No need to give the nosy neighbors any more ammunition if we can help it."

"Sounds good. See you later."

Chapter 6

Joe heard Ginny drive into the garage and close the door. He was at the door from the garage to the house as Ginny opened it.

"My very favorite detective," said Joe.

"What a coincidence, *my* very favorite detective is here also."

After an embrace and a lengthy, more-than-good-friends kiss, Joe and Ginny walked into the kitchen.

"OK, enough of that mushy stuff. For now. Time to order the pizza. All veggies for you, I suppose."

"Oh, Joe," said Ginny as she faked a swoon. "You know me so well."

Joe called his favorite local pizzeria, ordering one large pizza, half all veggies and half all meat, and two small Greek salads.

"Twenty-five minutes," said Joe. "I didn't want to order until you got here. In case you got delayed and I wound up sitting with one cold pizza."

"Cold pizza never slowed you down before. But thanks for waiting. What say a cold beer to while the time away?"

"Coming right up," said Joe as he opened the refrigerator, grabbed and opened two beers and handed one to Ginny.

They sat at the small kitchen table, drinking their beer and talking about the Wallerman case.

"Joe, where do you fall on the whole sanctuary city thing?"

"Good question. I've got mixed feelings. On the one hand, I think most of these illegal immigrants are good, hard-working people just looking for a better life for themselves and their family. Hard to fault them for that."

"True. But is it fair for them to illegally jump ahead of all the others who applied legally and are sitting and waiting their turn?"

"No. You're right about that. Also, despite most or almost all of them being good people, I'm sure a few bad apples, be they criminals or terrorists, are coming in among them."

"For sure. But I do agree with special rules for those illegals who were brought here as little kids by their parents. You can't blame the kids. It's the parents. But do you deport the parents and leave the children here?"

"See why I have mixed feelings?"

"Yes, I do. Also, these sanctuary cities let many of these illegals come out into the open, including paying taxes, getting a drivers' license and so on. And even being less afraid to talk to the cops if they see or know something."

"Yup, all good points. But whatever other towns and cities do, I hope Jasper Creek doesn't go that way."

"Why?"

"I don't want to have to choose, or have the department choose for me, whether I enforce the federal or the local laws. I want to be a good citizen of both the U.S. and Jasper Creek. So I hope they don't wind up having conflicting laws, forcing us to decide which to enforce and which to ignore."

"Wow. If nothing else, once we dig a little into this, it sure is a lot more complicated than you might initially think."

"Yeah, just like everything else."

Before they knew it, the pizza arrived and two minutes later, conversation stopped as they focused on the pizza. And beer.

Fifteen minutes later, they were sitting in Joe's small living room, Ginny on the couch and Joe on the side chair sitting next to the couch at 90 degrees.

"OK, Joe. Time to get to it."

"Yup. We gave ourselves three months to come up with a plan. We've already used up more than two weeks and we haven't made any progress."

"Well, I'm not sure. I think we've made a little. We agree that we're both tired of having to sneak around and not be seen in public. Driving an hour away just to go to a restaurant is getting to be a pain in the you-know-where."

"No argument on that, Ginny. And we confirmed our suspicion that the department policies don't cover this situation."

"Yeah. It clearly forbids relationships between a supervisor and a subordinate, but says nothing about two who just work together. That means the chief can use that 'conduct unbecoming' catchall policy to cover this if he wants it to."

"And who knows what the chief would decide. Hell, his decision might even be different from one day to the next."

"What if he forces us to choose between breaking up or stop being partners?"

"Talk about a choice between two lousy options. Hell, depending on how he slept the night before, he might even tell us we have to break up or that one us has to resign from the department."

"Joe, we gave ourselves 90 days to figure this out for a reason. We knew it was a tough problem. We shouldn't be too hard on ourselves for not having a solution after a couple of weeks."

"You're right, Ginny. Plus you forgot to mention the most important thing."

"Oh. What's that?"

Looking directly into Ginny's eyes, Joe said, "That we're super in love with each other."

"Joe, I didn't forget that. I never do. Not even for a minute. I didn't mention it because we both know it so well."

"OK, Ms. Diplomat, I'll give you a pass this time."

"Thank you. But back to the discussion. So where do we go from here?"

"I'm increasingly convinced that, despite all the risks, sooner or later we have to bite the bullet and tell the chief. That means he'll just decide. What he decides is the big question."

"You got that right. Anything we can do to increase the chances of him saying 'OK, no problemo?'"

"Ginny, you might be on to something. If we can solve this damn Wallerman case quickly, we could talk to him right after that. He'd be so pleased with the quick solving, and, therefore, how great a detective team we are and how much he needs us, he'd be more likely to say OK."

"Good point, Joe. But what if we don't solve the case quickly? Or we do, but he still says 'no way?'"

"Very negative thinking. But valid questions."

"Hey, what if we check with surrounding police departments that are about our size? To see if they have a policy on this and, if they do, what it is. And if they don't have a policy, how they usually decide things like this. Might give us a better idea of what the chief's unwritten policy would be. I could call and say I'm a college student doing a paper on this topic."

"Good idea, Ginny. And as long as you're not identified, we have nothing to lose."

"I can call from the public phone at the library tomorrow morning."

"OK. We made a little progress. Let's stop for now. But we still have to figure out what we do if the eventual answer is no and we have to end our partnering or our personal relationship, or one of us has to leave the department."

"Yeah, but let's leave those pretty thoughts for another day. Or night." Patting the couch cushion next to her, Ginny continued, "For now, why don't you join me here for a little TV before we head to the bedroom."

"Works for me."

Joe normally fell asleep almost as soon as his head hit the pillow. But that night he had trouble falling asleep. Not because of worry, but because he felt so lucky. He knew that Ginny had saved him. Who would have thought a Chicago kid like him, one who managed to grow up in the big city, become a cop, then a big-city detective who would eventually be kicked off the force because of drinking and just plain being obnoxious would wind up in a small Ohio town, working with someone like Ginny? Sleeping with her! In love with each other! He'd still been a mess when he'd arrived in Jasper Creek, having lost not just his job but his wife and little boy to that damn drunk driver. But Ginny had seen past what a mess he'd been. He still gets those feelings that being with Ginny is cheating on Lori, but that's happening less and less. He appreciates Ginny accepting those feelings and not trying to change his thinking or rush things. Now he and Ginny have to solve the department and chief problem.

At the same time, Ginny was lying silently but wide awake at Joe's side. They can't be sneaking around forever. But she sure wants to keep working with Joe. After her short marriage right out of high school, it looked like she'd be single forever. She was never interested in anyone again. Didn't even go on more than a few dates all those years. Was it her hatred for men because of the divorce? Or more fear of getting hurt again? Maybe both. Who knows? Then Joe came along. She recognized him as a rough, tough guy on the outside, but a real sweetie down deep. She feels like the luckiest person in the world. But she doesn't want them to have to sneak around for the rest of their lives. They have to figure out a way to go public and still be allowed to work together.

Eventually, both Joe and Ginny fell asleep.

Chapter 7

The next morning, the two detectives squeezed into the small shower together. After dressing and a quick breakfast of toast and coffee, they were on their way, Ginny to the library and Joe to the courthouse.

Arriving just as the library opened, Ginny walked to the rear section where she knew they kept the old newspapers for the past year and microfilm copies going back several years. Ginny started with the microfilm copies, since these allowed her to sort using Wallerman's name. She found several articles from his days as an ADA, a few dozen articles dealing with his defense attorney work and several more related to his town council activities. Rather than trying to read and analyze all of the articles, she selected each one and sent it to the large printer against the back wall. She then started going through the more recent newspapers that were stored in their original paper format. She quickly became frustrated with the inability to do an automated search for Wallerman, but she forced herself to get through the most recent three months of papers. She made copies of several articles. She then went to another section of the library where she looked up and wrote in her notebook the nonemergency phone numbers of four police departments in surrounding towns that she knew to be similar in size to Jasper Creek's department. Two hours and nine dollars later, Ginny left the library with a stack of newspaper page copies and several dollars of change she had gotten from the librarian.

She put the articles in her car, returned to the library lobby where a pay phone hung on the wall in one of the rear corners, and settled in to call the four police departments.

"Good morning. This is Officer Watson at the Carlisle Police Department. How can I be of help?"

"Good morning," said Ginny. "My name is Mary Hastings. I'm doing a research project for school. I'm surveying several police departments in Pennsylvania and Ohio. I'd like to talk with someone about your department's policies dealing with police officers who work together having a personal relationship."

"Hold on, Ms. Hastings. Let me transfer you to Sergeant Norman. She handles most of our administrative and personnel stuff and should be able to help you."

"OK. Thanks."

And then a minute later: "Hello. This is Sergeant Norman."

Ginny repeated her research-project story.

"Oh, that sounds like an interesting project. I'm happy to try to help. What do you want to know?"

"Does your department have a written policy about this?"

"Yes we do."

"And what does it say about two employees in the department having a personal relationship?"

"Well, the basic concept is to try to prevent risk or harm to the department and all its employees. So, for example, if the two employees don't work closely together, like say a detective and a traffic officer, the relationship is OK so long as they don't make others in the department feel uncomfortable. Like if they're hugging and kissing all day long."

"That makes sense. What if they do work more closely together?"

"First off, if one is a supervisor of the other, personal relationships are not allowed. For other situations, the chief makes the call on a case-by-case basis. So let's say it's two patrol officers who are partners, or two detectives. Like before, it won't be allowed if they make others feel uncomfortable. But more important, it won't be allowed if it risks safety."

"Like how?"

"Let's say one of the two is always getting his or her partner to do less risky things, like covering the back door. That means other officers will more often have to step up front. Or if they're so worried about each other that they lose focus on the job at hand."

"Yikes. Those must be tough calls for the chief to make."

"Yes, they are. And, when in doubt, he errs on the side of protecting the department and its employees, not the relationship."

"Can you give me some idea of how often this comes up and how the chief usually decides?"

"It happens more often than you might think. Partners, whether they're patrol officers or detectives, spend more time with each other than with anyone else. They get to know each other very well. And usually, based on all that they see and do, they develop a close bond and find that they think alike. It's difficult for many cops to relate well with civilians. Only other cops really understand what cops go through and have to face every day. Unfortunately, all this often results in married folks cheating on their spouse. In addition to the stress of the job, this is another, but less talked about, reason for the high divorce rate among cops."

"I see."

"But to answer your question more specifically, since we put this policy into effect about seven years ago, we've probably had about five situations where the chief had to play Solomon."

"And how did he decide?"

"I don't have hard statistics on this, but he probably made them end the relationship about two-thirds of the time."

"And what if they don't or don't want to?"

"In one case, one of them was able to take a different job in the department to resolve the issue. But we're a small department. We don't have many possibilities like that. If we don't, one of them has to leave the department. They can decide which one leaves, or if they don't decide, the chief will."

"Wow. That sounds pretty insensitive."

"It may sound that way, but you realize it's not when you recognize that the chief's first priority is the safety and morale of all the department employees."

"Do you think most police departments have similar policies?"

"Not sure, but I'd think so. We checked around when we were developing our policy. Back then, many of the departments had no policy at all. The few that did had policies similar to this. Not surprising, most of the large departments had a written policy, whereas most of the smaller departments didn't."

"Thank you very much, Sergeant. This has been very helpful."

"You're very welcome. Good luck with your project."

"Thank you. Goodbye."

"Goodbye."

Ginny finished writing her notes about the phone call and then called the other three departments. One had a policy much like Carlisle's. The other two had no written policy; the chief decided on a case-by-case basis. One of these last two volunteered that the chief's decision was more likely to be negative if he found out that the relationship had been going on secretly for an extended period.

Hearing that, Ginny was more worried than ever about her relationship with Joe. And she had no clearer idea as to what to do about telling the chief, and how long to wait before telling him.

By then, it was close to noon. Ginny returned to her car and headed back to the station.

Chapter 8

While Ginny had been hard at work in the library, Joe visited the County Prosecutor's Office.

After a short wait in the outer office, Prosecutor Porter came out to meet him.

"Good morning, Detective. What can I do for you? And how's the Wallerman case coming?"

"Morning, Charles. Your two questions are closely related. We're plugging along on the case, but could use your help on one item."

"What's that? Happy to help all we can."

"Great. One of the several avenues we're pursuing is that his homicide was related to his assistant prosecuting attorney days."

"You'll be busy. That takes in a lot of time and a lot of potential suspects."

"We know. But we can greatly reduce the number. His APA work ended almost 20 years ago. It's unlikely that something that happened that long ago led to his being killed now. Unless—"

"Unless?"

"Unless the killer was unable to kill him sooner."

"Like he was in prison?"

"Exactly, or perhaps living overseas. Or being in a coma, or in a mental hospital for 15 years."

"OK, I get your point. How can we help?"

"I know that all of your cases going back almost to Noah are computerized."

"Well, yes, almost. But not quite that far back."

"We need someone to go through your computer files to get all the cases where Wallerman was the APA. Then, for each 'injured party,' we need to identify all those who weren't available until recently."

"What do you mean by 'injured party?'"

"Either a defendant who was convicted and sent to prison or the victim of a defendant who was found not guilty. Or family members or close friends of these defendants and victims."

"Jeez, Joe. Do you realize how many cases Wallerman must have handled? He was here for five years."

"I know. That's why we need someone in your department who knows how to meander around your computer system. Then once these people are identified, he or she needs to search other files and the Internet to find those who were out of commission, so to say, until recently."

"Hmm. Interesting idea. I think I've got just the person who can help."

"I bet it's someone young to be able to do all the computer stuff."

"Exactly. Jane Daniels is an intern we recently brought on. I think she's got the right skills for this. And it'll be a good way for her to get some info on the history of the department. Come on, I'll introduce you to her."

Joe followed Porter to Daniels' cubbyhole in the back corner. After introductions, Joe described what he was looking for. Daniels clearly grasped the concept and expressed confidence that she could manage her way through the prosecutor's and other databases. Joe was pleased and said he'd check back in a couple of days to see how she was progressing.

Joe thanked them both and headed back to his office. Along the way, he stopped at Patrol Division, only to learn that their surveillance had not found any of Wallerman's neighbors who had seen or heard anything; there also weren't any cameras in the area.

Joe returned to his desk. Twenty minutes later Ginny returned to hers.

"Hey, Partner. How'd you make out this morning?"

"Pretty well," said Joe. "How about I fill you in over lunch? Then perhaps we can head over to the law firm where Wallerman used to work and then to his current law office."

"Sounds like a good idea. And I can fill you in about my morning as well."

Joe took a look at the local phonebook, called Dewey, Cavanaugh and Williams and made a two o'clock appointment to meet with Robert Cavanaugh, Senior.

Five minutes later, Joe and Ginny were out the door and on their way to Sancho's Taco Shop.

Chapter 9

Between bites of his burrito, Joe filled Ginny in about his visits to the prosecutor's office and the Patrol Division. Ginny then gave Joe a brief summary of her library visit as well as her calls to surrounding police departments.

"Sounds like we've got a bunch of newspaper reading to do."

"Not to mention a bunch more strategizing about us and the chief."

"That's for sure. So after lunch, let's head over to Wallerman's old law firm."

After finishing lunch, a five-minute walk took Joe and Ginny to the elevator and up to the third floor of an old, but well-kept, four-story office building.

A right turn off the elevator and the first office on their left had "Dewey, Cavanaugh and Williams" stenciled on the opaque glass door. Joe and Ginny entered and walked up to the attractive young receptionist sitting at a desk near the rear wall.

"Hi. We're Detectives Harris and McFarland. We have a meeting with Mr. Cavanaugh."

"Senior or junior?"

"Senior."

"One moment, please."

The receptionist made a quick call, hung up and said,

"Follow me, please. I'll take you to Mr. Cavanaugh's office."

And she did. After introductions and an offer and refusal of coffee, Joe and Ginny were sitting on a plush red couch against the side wall of Cavanaugh's office, and Cavanaugh was in an easy chair facing them across a coffee table.

"So what can I help you with, Detectives?"

"We'd like to get some information about Carl Wallerman."

"That's what I assumed this'd be about. What a shame. Who'd do something like that?"

"That's exactly what we're working on," said Ginny. "We assume you knew him well when he used to work here."

"Most definitely. In fact, I was the one who proposed we hire him. We were a much smaller firm back then. We all worked closely together and knew each other quite well."

"We know it was a lot of years ago, but we're trying to determine if any cases he worked on back then might be related to his killing," said Ginny.

"Wow, that's a tough one. As you probably know, he was a criminal defense attorney and handled many cases."

"Do any stick in your memory where his client was found guilty and threatened him?" asked Joe.

"Or where a victim threatened him after he got his client off?" added Ginny.

"Well, all of us on the criminal side of the practice have received threats. But these don't amount to much. They're usually made in the heat of the moment, right after the trial ends, and then they're quickly forgotten."

"Understood. Any unusual situations you can remember in Mr. Wallerman's case would be appreciated."

"Let me think."

Then, a couple of minutes later: "No. I'm sorry. Nothing comes to mind. It was several years ago, you know."

"Yes, we do. Mr. Cavanaugh, here are our cards," said Ginny as she and Joe each handed him a business card. "We'd appreciate you discussing this with some of the others who were here when Mr. Wallerman was, and calling us if anything along these lines is remembered."

"OK. I will. But don't be too optimistic."

"No need to worry about that, Sir," said Joe with a smile. "We're never too optimistic. We're cops."

And with that, Joe and Ginny said their goodbyes and left.

Chapter 10

Ten minutes later, they entered the second-floor office of the firm of Carl Wallerman, Attorney At Law.

There was no one sitting at the large wooden desk in the outer office, but one of the two doors behind the desk was partway open. Joe and Ginny opened the door wider and walked into what obviously had been Wallerman's office. There was an attractive middle-aged woman standing at a file cabinet with her back to the door.

As quietly as possible, Joe said, "Hello."

With a screech and a nervous jump, the woman turned around. "Yes? My God, you scared me half to death."

"Sorry," said Ginny. "We're detectives investigating the death of Mr. Wallerman."

And with that, the woman began sobbing. Judging by her red face and red eyes, she clearly already had been doing a lot of crying. When her sobbing slowed down, she managed to say, "Sorry. I still can't believe what happened."

"Yes. You have our deepest sympathies," said Ginny.

"I'm Mr. Wallerman's paralegal. I'm trying to go through all our open cases and figure out what to do. But I have no idea. Mostly, I'm calling other attorneys to get them to take over the various cases."

"That sounds like a sensible approach. May we sit down and talk for a few minutes?"

"Sure. Let's go sit around the conference table over there."

Once seated, Ginny began. "I'm Detective Harris and this is Detective McFarland."

"Hi. I'm Margaret Radner. I've been with Mr. Cavanaugh ever since he opened this practice almost 13 years ago. I'm just totally lost right now. It's like a terrible nightmare that I can't wake up from. Fortunately, Mr. Collins said I can call him whenever I have a question or need help."

"Mr. Collins?" asked Ginny.

"Yes, I'm sorry. David Collins. He and Mr. Wallerman went to law school together. Mr. Wallerman made him executor of his estate."

"Is Mr. Collins here in Jasper Creek?" asked Joe.

"Yes. His office is over on Market Street. You've probably never dealt with him. He doesn't handle criminal cases. Just civil stuff, like contracts and estate planning."

"OK. Thank you. We'll arrange to speak with him," said Ginny.

"He called me the same day it was on the news. He told me that he was the executor. He said it would take him a while to get everything sorted out. He wanted me to stay working here for a couple of months to help organize and shut things down. He also asked me to arrange all the details of the funeral. So sad that Mr. Wallerman had no family to even do that. Mr. Collins said the estate would continue my current salary and benefits for that period."

"We understand," said Ginny. "One of the avenues we're pursuing is that the killer might have been one of Mr.

Wallerman's past or current clients. Perhaps someone who got very upset, perhaps threatening Mr. Wallerman, when he or she was found guilty."

"Mr. Wallerman had his fair share of those. I mean, you have to assume that many or maybe even most of his clients were guilty. He couldn't get several of them off."

"Can you think of any specific ones?" asked Joe. "Most likely, it was either a recent case, where the client's family or friend acted while the client was in prison, or it could have been an older case where the client has just recently been released from prison."

"Oh, I see where you're going. Those are the only ways one of them would have killed him now."

"Exactly," said Ginny. "Do any cases come to mind?"

"Not immediately. But if you give me a day or two, I can go through the files and prepare a list for you. As a small firm, we never computerized all this stuff. But we keep, or I guess I should say kept, very good files and records."

"That would be very helpful. How about letters he's received? Death threats?"

"Mr. Wallerman saved all those type of letters. Some were related to his law practice, but a fair number were related to his work on the town council."

"Oh, that reminds me. Here's some mail for Mr. Waller-man that we picked up when we were at the town council offices. We can't open them without a warrant, but you can."

"Joe shook out the few letters from a plastic file folder onto the conference table in front of Radner. He stopped her as she began to reach for the first letter. "Hold on,

Ms. Radner. Please put these disposable gloves on. Just in case one of these letters is relevant to our investigation and there are fingerprints on the letter."

"Oh, OK. But this all looks like junk mail to me."

Radner put on the gloves that Joe handed her and then proceeded to open the letters. Sure enough, one was an offer for a credit card, one for auto insurance, a coupon for a new pizza parlor in town and a list of upcoming performances at the local theater.

"Well, you were right on about this mail. How about those previous letters that Mr. Wallerman received?"

"Yes, over here," said Radner, as she got up and led the detectives to a bookcase across the room. "As you can see, Mr. Wallerman had a great sense of humor." On one of the shelves were three metal trays, each with a label: "Loves Me," "Doesn't Care" and "Hates Me." The first two trays were each about half full. The "Hates Me" tray was filled almost to the top.

"Each of these letters has the envelope stapled to it for the return address, when there was one. I'd guess almost half of them relate to the law practice and the rest to his town council work. Oh, I'm going to miss him so much," said Radner as she started crying again.

"We understand. Please take care of yourself. We're going to borrow these three trays of letters, if that's OK."

"Sure, you can take them. And I assume you know that two of your colleagues were here Monday afternoon and borrowed Mr. Wallerman's computer, though he hardly ever used it. They also checked his phone for voicemail messages."

"Yes, we're aware of that," said Ginny.

"I'll start going through our files this evening."

"That would be great. Here are our cards. If you could call us by Friday, or Monday if need be, we'd be most appreciative."

"OK."

"Thank you. Also, please let us know once the funeral arrangements are set. And again, we're very sorry for your loss."

"Yes, I'll call you. And thank you."

Joe and Ginny walked back to their offices.

Ginny had a phone message to call the coroner. She called him back and had a brief discussion, during which Ginny mostly listened.

Hanging up, Ginny said, "OK, Joe. The autopsy by the state confirmed everything the coroner had told us on a preliminary basis at the crime scene. But it didn't provide any additional information. The two shots were definitely 10mm, and either could have been the kill shot. And no change to his time estimate, between eight and midnight."

"OK. At least the caliber and the time period are confirmed."

"Yup."

"And BCI will be checking the striations on the bullets versus their and the fed's databases, but a match is a long shot."

"Yeah. And probably a long time from now. What's next?"

"I'm going to call that estate lawyer and try to set up an appointment for the morning," said Joe.

"Good idea."

Joe made the call, spoke to Collins' executive assistant

and arranged for a meeting the next day at 10 a.m. Joe and Ginny cleaned up their desks. Each of them answered a couple of phone messages, and then headed out the door.

"Joe, how about dinner at my place for a change? We're almost always going to your house."

"Sounds like a plan. Why don't you head on home. I'll swing by the supermarket for some stuff to eat. And, more importantly, some beer and wine."

"Can't argue with that."

"Sure. Take one of your beloved bathtub soaks while I slave over a hot supermarket shelf."

"Will do. That bath sounds great. Thanks."

"My pleasure. See you soon."

Ginny raced home and was soaking in the tub before Joe reached the supermarket. Joe parked, entered and grabbed a cart just inside the door. He was in and out in 10 minutes with two pork chops, sweet potatoes, frozen peas and carrots and a frozen apple pie. Plus, a bottle of California merlot and an ice-cold six-pack of one of the local craft beers.

Reaching Ginny's apartment complex, Joe parked at the far end of the parking lot. The less attention he drew to himself the better.

Answering the doorbell, Ginny looked totally refreshed. Joe entered the apartment, closed the door and gave her a long, deep kiss, all the while holding the two bags from the supermarket.

"I don't know how you do it. After the long day we put in, you look as fresh as you do first thing in the morning."

"That's my magic bath. You ought to give it a try."

"Yeah. Sure. That's all we need. You'd have to call 9-1-1 to help get me out of the tub."

"OK. Your loss. What's for dinner?"

"Beer and wine."

"That's nice. Anything else?"

"Oh, yeah. Apple pie."

"That's nice, too. Anything else?"

"Oh, yeah. I forgot. Pork chops, sweet potatoes and veggies."

"Hmm. Sounds lovely. Who's the cook tonight? You or me?"

"I developed the menu and did the purchasing. So you can do the cooking and we'll share the washing."

"Sounds fair."

"I'll put everything on the counter in the kitchen. Does the chef want wine or beer while she's cooking?"

"I'll go with beer while cooking, then wine while eating."

"Got it. I'll do the same."

They were eating before they knew it.

"Boy, that was sad."

"What? My cooking?"

"No. No. Sorry. I was thinking about Wallerman's paralegal. She seemed devastated. Like her whole life revolved around him."

"You're right. I bet it's one of those things where she was deeply in love with him. She never said a word, and he never had any idea."

"Sounds like a mushy TV movie, but I think you may be right. Hope we never get like that."

"Well, our whole lives may revolve around each other and we may be deeply in love, but at least we both know it."

"That's true."

"Joe, we need to talk more about my calls with those police departments this morning, and what it means about us and the chief. But I'm brain-dead now. How about we do the dishes, watch a little TV and then hit the sack? We can talk tomorrow."

"Works for me."

Ninety minutes later they were curled together, fast asleep under Ginny's quilt.

Chapter 11

Joe and Ginny were up and ready for work early
the next morning.

"I'm sure not looking forward to today," said
Joe.

"Why's that?"

"I bet we're going to spend most of the day reading
through the zillion letters we picked up from the council
and from Wallerman's office."

"But the good news is, when you get totally bored, you
can switch to looking through the copies of all the newspaper articles I got at the library."

"Oh, joy of joys. I think I'd rather be a TV detective
than a real detective. They never have to spend their time
doing boring, brain-numbing stuff like this."

"True. But I have a great idea. How about we plan on an
early afternoon visit to that council lady who agreed with
the vic on that sanctuary stuff?"

"Great idea. That'll at least give us a nice break. When
we get to the office, why don't you track her down and try
to schedule something?"

"Will do. Now it's off to the station. In two cars. I'm
outta here."

"OK. I'll be right behind you."

With a hug and a kiss, Ginny was off. Five minutes later,
Joe followed.

At their desks, each with a cup of fairly fresh, hot

coffee, they started scanning through the piles of letters. Joe took the council letters. Ginny started on Wallerman's "Hate Me" pile. About an hour in, Ginny took a break to schedule the meeting with Elizabeth Gould, the other council member. After getting her phone number from Betsy at the council office, Ginny called and set up a meeting with Gould for one o'clock that afternoon. Gould indicated she owned a small Internet company that she ran from home, so they could meet there. She gave Ginny her address.

After another 15 minutes of letter reading, Ginny suddenly sat up straight. "Joe, I think I might have something."

"What is it?"

"I gotta read you this letter to Wallerman."

"Go for it."

"Dear Scumbag, How can you defend those scumbags? And don't give me that horseshit about everyone being entitled to a lawyer. That's not true for most of your scumbag clients. I bet you'd see it differently if you or your wife or daughter was the victim. But what can you expect from a scumbag lawyer?" You'll get yours one of these days."

"Do I detect a bit of hostility there?"

"Yeah. Just a bit."

"Sounds pretty threatening. This guy, assuming it's a guy, is pretty pissed about one of Wallerman's cases."

"Yeah. He or a family member may have been a victim of one of Wallerman's clients."

"Is there a date?" asked Joe. "No signature or return address, I assume."

"No date or return address. But there is a name. Looks like Paul Harris or Harkness. Hard to read. This would be a nice one to interview."

"Yup. Right at the top of our list."

After about another hour of going through letters, Ginny said, "Let's fill each other in on what we've got so far. Then we need to head to Collins' office. It's about a 10-minute drive from here."

"Good idea. I can't read any more now anyhow. My summary is pretty brief. I'm about halfway through the pile of letters to the town council. I pulled out about a half dozen for us to review and possibly follow up on. Most of the letters were dry, mundane mumblings about a million minor things. A neighbor's tree overhanging a guy's property. A complaint that property taxes are too high. A demand that the library let you keep a book out for a month rather than three weeks. And on and on. There were also a few letters mixed in thanking or praising the council for some inconsequential decision they made. The few letters I pulled out were clearly written by people very upset about something and, in a few cases, included general threats."

"In addition to that Harris or Harkness letter, going through the rest of Wallerman's hate mail, I pulled a lot more out. Probably about 20 percent of the letters. Most of the so-called hate letters were more minor-dislike letters. I pulled any of them where I could feel the anger or emotion of the writer. We may have to go back later and check more of the letters, but I think I'm getting most of those that deserve top priority," Ginny said, pointing to the smaller pile.

"OK. Sounds like we're making progress. Let's put this aside for now. Time to head to that lawyer's office."

"Right on. I just need to make a pit stop on the way out."

"Ditto. And, by the way, that's something else that TV detectives never do."

A short while later, Ginny pulled into the small parking lot in front of Collins' office. The office was on the second floor of an old, large house that had been subdivided into office space for five or six tenants. They walked in, went up the stairs and entered Collins' office. Joe introduced Ginny and himself to the receptionist.

"Yes, hello, Detectives. I'm the one you spoke with yesterday. I'll let Mr. Collins know you're here. He's expecting you."

"Thanks," said Joe.

Two minutes later, Collins came out and greeted them. After introductions, they walked through a doorway into Collins' office and sat down. Joe and Ginny accepted Collins' offer of coffee, and he poured cups for them and for himself from the coffee pot sitting on a marble counter behind his desk.

"Mr. Collins, we'd like to talk with you about Mr. Wallerman."

"Yes. Yes. Of course. What a terrible shame. Who would do something like that?"

"That's exactly what we're working on," said Joe. "Any idea who disliked him or who he was having a big disagreement with?"

"No idea. But you need to understand, Carl and I weren't really close. We attended law school together, but were never buddy-buddy. We'd see each other maybe two or three times a year, mostly at bar association events. And once in a while we'd bump into each other in town or at the courthouse. Plus, of course, when we worked on his estate. When we first set up his estate plan, and then we'd review and modify it each time he got married or divorced. Other than that, I really don't know many details of Carl's private life."

"We understand that you're the executor of his estate," said Ginny.

"Yes, that's correct. Executor of his estate and trustee of his trust."

"Can you tell us about the heirs to the estate?"

"Yes. But I'd appreciate you keeping it quiet for a week or so. I haven't told the heirs yet. I want to determine the dollar amounts so I can tell them everything at once."

"Understood. I don't think we'll be needing to tell anyone in the next week or so," said Joe.

"This kind of information often says a lot about a person's life. That's surely the case with poor Carl," said Collins as he slowly rotated his head from side to side.

"Can you be more specific?" asked Ginny.

"Sure. Sorry. Each of his former wives, if you can believe it, will get 25 percent, his paralegal, Margaret Radner, will get 25 percent and the remaining 25 percent will be split among a handful of charities."

"I see," said Joe.

"It indicates a rather barren life to me. The closest and dearest people to him are two ex-wives and an employee. But it's not for me to judge."

"When do you intend to inform the heirs, Mr. Collins?" asked Joe.

"In about a week. I want to first tally up all the monetary assets, then get estimates for selling his house, his car and his practice. Then I need to estimate the costs the estate will incur: the funeral, final tax payments and the temporary continued employment of Ms. Radner. I told her to keep working for the next couple of months to help me shut everything down and sell off or donate everything. She's also working on the funeral arrangements. I've found that it helps to give the heirs right up front a fairly accurate estimate of how much they should expect. Otherwise, they start dreaming about totally unrealistic amounts and then are unhappy when reality sets in."

"Yes, I can understand that," said Ginny. "Can you give us a preliminary estimate of the amount?"

"Don't hold me to this, but I'd estimate that, when you combine the assets in his trust and those assets covered by his will, and then subtract the expenses the estate will incur, the total will be between $1.5 and $2.5 million."

"I think that's it for now," said Joe. "Here are our business cards. Please call if you think of anything else. And we'll be back in touch if we have more questions."

"Sure enough."

A few minutes later, Joe and Ginny were back in Ginny's car.

"Wow. Those ex-wives and his paralegal are gonna be three very surprised and very happy ladies."

"They sure are. It also earns them positions high on our possible suspects list. They'll each get at least $375 K. A lot more if the estate has two and a half mil, not just one and a half. That's one heck of a motive. Surely a lot more attractive than ongoing alimony, or even salary, over the next umpteen years."

"But it's only a motive if they knew they were an heir before he was killed."

"Very true. Ginny, are you sure you don't have any long-lost, millionaire uncles who're going to leave you a few mil when they kick the bucket?"

"Fraid not, Joe. You're the closest thing I have to a gravy train."

"You're in pretty bad shape then. Sorry to hear that. But I think I'll stick with you anyhow."

"My lucky day."

After a quick Burger King lunch stop, they headed to Gould's house.

"Joe, do you think she's in any danger?"

"Hard to tell. Until we know that the killing was related to Wallerman's sanctuary city efforts, and then that Gould's involvement was known, there's not much we can do. When we get back, I'll talk to Patrol and have them increase their frequency of driving by her place. I'll also see if they can have a car sit in front of her house when they're not responding to calls. But that's about it."

"Well, it's something. If nothing else, it might put her mind a bit at ease."

"Right."

Chapter 12

A few minutes later, Ginny parked in front of the house. Ginny noted how the small house had a very cozy look to it. The light brown wood shingles along the front, with dark brown shutters at all the windows on both the first and second floors, blended nicely with the covered porch running the full width of the house. Joe and Ginny walked up the brick walkway and rang the front doorbell.

Elizabeth Gould opened the door. "Yes?"

"Hello. Mrs. Gould? I'm Detective Harris. We spoke a few hours ago. And this is Detective McFarland. May we come in?"

"Yes, of course. Please come in. Let's go sit in the sunroom. It should be bright and cheery today."

Joe and Ginny followed her toward the back of the house. Joe couldn't help noting to himself, *Pretty well-preserved.* She was probably in her mid-50s, but with the right makeup and clothing, could pass for being in her early 40s. She had a nice, trim figure, whose short skirt showed off her long, thin legs. Her hair, no doubt salon-colored, was long, dark brown, and sexy. She stood tall and carried herself well. When Ginny mentioned she was a widow, Joe had pictured a 65-year-old, chubby, gray-haired woman. So much for assumptions. *If it weren't for Ginny,* Joe thought, *I could get interested in local politics.*

As they entered the sunroom, Gould exclaimed, "Oh! Adrianna. I didn't realize you were in here. Sorry."

"Not a problem, Mom. I was just doing a little reading while soaking up the sun through the window. I'll go into the study."

"Thank you, Dear. These are Detectives Harris and McFarland," said Gould as she pointed to each of the detectives. "And, Detectives, this is my daughter, Adrianna."

"Hello."

"Pleased to meet you."

Joe's mind went into overdrive again. *Now that's one beautiful lady.* Probably what her mother looked like 25 years ago, except the younger generation was an improved model: straight black hair, pretty face with a perfectly straight nose, a delightful figure and a few inches height on her mother. *Come on, Joe, get your mind back to the task at hand.*

With a swish of her skirt, Adrianna, book in hand, was gone from the room.

"Your daughter seems lovely," said Ginny.

"Thank you. Yes, she is. We've always been close, and we've gotten closer since my husband passed a few years ago. Please, have a seat."

"Sorry to hear about your husband," said Ginny as the three of them sat down. "But it must be comforting and helpful to have your daughter living with you."

"Oh, Adrianna doesn't really live here. She's just staying here temporarily. She and her husband have been going through a couple of rough patches recently. Like the previous ones, they'll work this one out. In any event, I'm sure you'd rather get to the subject you mentioned when you called. Poor Carl. We're all shocked. I can't imagine why anyone would want to kill him."

"Yes, that's what we're trying to find out. The who and the why," said Joe. "Any thoughts? Any disagreements he had with anyone?"

"Not that I'm aware of."

"We heard that you and he were the only two council members favoring Jasper Creek becoming a sanctuary city, or town I guess I should say."

"Yes, that's correct. The other council members are either against it or undecided. Carl and I were working to gradually change their minds. Now with Carl gone, the odds are worse than ever."

"Mrs. Gould, do you think that effort could possibly be a motive for Carl's murder?" asked Joe.

"What? I doubt it. I mean some people are strongly against it, but I can't believe enough so to commit murder."

"Yes, well that's just one of several areas we're looking into. Have you received any hate mail or threats because of your position on this issue?"

"Yes, some. And I know that Carl has too. And I've also gotten similar letters for other town council matters. But we didn't take any of that seriously."

"Do you have those letters you received?"

"Yes. Would you like to see them?"

"Yes," said Ginny. "In fact, we'd like to borrow them for a while."

"Sure. Give me a minute. I'll get them now."

Gould walked out of the room and returned a few

minutes later with about 25 letters clipped together. "Here you are."

"Thank you," said Ginny as she took the letters.

"My God, do you think I'm next on the murderer's list?" asked Gould as she covered her mouth with her right hand.

"Let's not get ahead of ourselves. This is only one of several possible motives for Mr. Wallerman's death. Let's not worry until we learn more. But, just to be sure, we're arranging for the patrol cars assigned to this area to drive by your house on a more frequent than normal basis. And whenever they can, one of them will be parked in front of your house."

"Oh. OK. Thank you."

"Thank you, Mrs. Gould. We may contact you again if we have more questions. And we'll return these letters to you," said Ginny.

"Goodbye, Mrs. Gould. And please say goodbye to your daughter for us," said Joe.

"I will," said Gould as she led them to the front door and opened it. Back in the car, Ginny headed back toward PD headquarters.

"That was a useful visit," said Joe.

"In terms of you eyeballing two attractive women? Or were there also other useful aspects?"

"What? What do you mean?"

"Joe, you're in trouble. I know you too well. All I had to do was watch where your eyes were aimed. And I bet I can even accurately guess your thoughts."

"Ginny, I—"

"Joe, no need to deny it. I'm fine with it. I've got no problem, as long as you're only window shopping."

"Well, OK then. You've got nothing to worry about. No matter how much I window shop, I won't be buying anything."

"Works for me. But I do need to point out that you're almost old enough to be the daughter's father."

"Boy, you sure know how to hurt a guy. Anyhow, as long as I'm just window shopping, I can check out the Rolls Royce dealership even though a Rolls is way out of my league. Plus, I don't want to be accused of age discrimination," said Joe with a smile.

"Fair enough."

"OK. Enough said. Let's get our heads back on the case."

"Deal. Back to our desks for more letter and newspaper reading?"

"OK. I'm with you."

And Joe and Ginny were soon reading through the letters they had gotten from the town council, from Wallerman's office and from Gould.

About 2:30, Ginny got a call from Radner.

After the call, Ginny turned to Joe. "That was Wallerman's paralegal. The funeral is set for Monday morning at 10. First at the church on Fifth and then the burial at Mount Holly."

"As usual, we'll attend. One of these days, we'll solve a case by identifying the perp at the vic's funeral."

Around four o'clock, Ginny put down her pen, leaned back in her chair and said, "OK, I give up for today. I can't read another letter without going crazy. Plus, my eyes are burning."

"Tell me about it."

"I'm ready to call it a day. We can finish up the rest of the letters as well as the newspaper articles tomorrow. We also have to track down that Harris or Harkness letter writer, the sooner the better."

"Works for me. Whaddaya want to do tonight?"

"Joe, nothing personal, but I'd like to just go home, soak in my tub, have an early dinner and go to bed. You OK with that?"

"Yeah, I'm pretty pooped myself. I'd rather spend the night together, but I do understand. And I like the fact that our relationship is good enough that you can feel free to tell me to get lost and I gracefully accept it."

"Thanks, Joe. You're an angel. But, just to be clear, I have difficulty describing anything you do as being graceful."

"Well, you haven't seen me do ballet yet. Wait 'til I get my light blue tutu back from the cleaners."

"That would be a sight. I can just picture it. OK, I'm out of here. See you tomorrow. Love ya."

"Yeah, me too. Have a good night. See you in the morning."

Joe stayed about 15 minutes after Ginny left to straighten out the piles of letters on his desk. He wanted to be sure that in the morning he could tell which ones he had identified as being worthy of a more detailed look, which ones he had passed on and which ones he still had to read.

Chapter 13

Both Joe and Ginny were back at their desks by 7:30 the next morning.

"Morning. How was your tub soaking and your night's sleep?"

"Both were super. I feel like a new woman today."

"Great. I feel good also. Ready to get back to the letters and the articles? And we definitely need to find out who that Harris or Harkness guy is."

"Sounds like a plan."

Around 9:15, Joe got a call from the crime scene lab. They had just finished their analysis of Wallerman's home phone voicemail messages, as well as just about everything on his cellphone and PC. They said that they didn't find anything relevant to the investigation, but the detectives were welcome to see for themselves. Joe and Ginny went downstairs and spent about 45 minutes listening and looking, only to agree with the crime scene techs' opinion.

"Thanks, guys," said Ginny. "Sorry to say, but we agree with you."

"Yeah. The killer clearly didn't leave a message or e-mail identifying himself as the killer. Too bad."

"OK, Joe. Guess we have to go back upstairs and continue our investigation the old-fashioned, step-by-step way."

Back upstairs, they finished going through all the letters a little before 11 o'clock.

"Ginny, let's summarize what we've pulled out from these letters. From all the letters to the town council, I put aside seven I think we should look into. For some of them, I can't even say why I pulled them out. I just ran with my gut."

"I did the same thing with Wallerman's hate mail. Unfortunately, I've got almost 20, 18 to be exact, including that one from Harris or Harkness, for us to look into further."

"Well, we've got quite a few. But, it's actually fewer than I feared when we began."

"True. Happily, I only pulled three from Gould's hate-mail pile. And one of the three is exactly the same as a letter to Wallerman. So Gould's letters really only add two new players."

"Still a lot of names to check out, but I'm sure we'll be able to eliminate a bunch pretty quickly. The letter writer's dead, or in prison, or severely handicapped or whatever."

"I hope so. From what I've read, that Harris or Harkness letter to Wallerman still stands out as numero uno."

"Full agreement."

"OK. Joe, I'll start searching for him. Why don't you start trying to eliminate some of the other letters we pulled aside?"

"Sounds like a plan. And let's not forget that we still have to work through all those newspaper articles you found."

"Don't worry. After all my effort at the library, I won't let us forget them."

"OK, Ginny. But the letters first. I'm not up to reading the newspaper articles now."

"OK. I'll defer to your request because of your advanced age."

"Ouch. But I'll take a victory any way I can."

One and a half hours later, they were both done.

"OK, Ginny. Whaddaya got?"

"I made some progress on our favorite letter writer. Checking various files and websites, as well as phone directories for Jasper Creek and surrounding towns, I came up with three Paul Harrises and two Paul Harknesses."

"Great. And I made some progress on the other letters we selected. Surprisingly, this work was kind of fun. Checking each writer out on the Internet and in our various databases, I was able to whittle our 27 suspicious letters to 17. Two of the writers are dead and one's in prison. One writer is 82 years old, one's in a long-term care facility and one had pictures on Facebook of him being at a family reunion in Chicago when the homicide was committed. There were photos of two of them being overseas at the time of the murder. And two have moved out of state, one to California and one to Florida."

"OK, Joe. Down to 17. That's a nice step forward."

"Yup. What say we go grab lunch and then go find our Paul Harris or Harkness?"

"Works for me."

After their routine lunch at Sancho's, Joe and Ginny got into Ginny's car and began their Harris/Harkness search. The first two Paul Harrises were quickly eliminated from the suspect list. The first one looked to be in his late 80s and was barely able to walk, even with the use of a walker. The second one had a clear alibi: He was out of town the night of the homicide and had receipts and witnesses to prove it. As soon as they returned to Ginny's car, Joe called the three witnesses. One didn't answer, but the other two confirmed the four-day fishing trip to Michigan.

Their next stop was at one of the Paul Harkness apartments. He wasn't home, but his wife told Joe and Ginny where he worked.

Ginny parked in front of the Jasper Electronics store. Both detectives got out of the car and walked up to the Customer Service counter.

"Hello," said Ginny. "We're Detectives Harris and McFarland. We'd like to speak with one of your employees, Paul Harkness."

"One minute, please. He's in the back, putting away a bunch of inventory that we received this morning. I'll have him join us."

The customer service clerk spoke into a microphone she wore around her neck. Five minutes later, a short, muscular man, about 40 years old, approached Ginny and Joe.

"I'm Paul Harkness. You wanna see me?"

"Yes, we do, Mr. Harkness. Is there someplace we can talk privately?"

"Probably. But here's fine with me. Whaddaya want?"

"Mr. Harkness, we're detectives with the Jasper Creek Police Department."

"Well, goody for you. Again, whaddaya want?"

"We'd like to talk with you about the letter you wrote to Mr. Wallerman. You recall it?"

"Yeah. Sure. But that was a couple of months ago. What about it?"

"Mr. Wallerman was killed Monday."

"So I heard. But I'm not in mourning."

"Mr. Harkness," said Joe, "your letter to him was rather threatening."

"Not in my view. But, anyhow, if you think that means I killed him, you better go back to detective school for a refresher."

"Mr. Harkness, where were you Monday night?"

"Sorry, but that's none of your business."

"Well, you happen to be wrong about that," said Joe. "You can either answer our questions here, or we can continue downtown."

"Downtown would be fine with me. Putting all the inventory crap away is a pain."

"OK, then, let's go for a ride."

"Sure. Let me just tell the fine folks here that I'll be gone for a bit."

Harkness told the customer service rep to tell his boss that he'd be out for a couple of hours, "helping the cops on one of their cases."

With Harkness in the back seat of Ginny's car, Ginny and Joe returned to the station and joined Harkness in one of the small interrogation rooms. Joe read Harkness his Miranda rights, after which he recorded the entire discussion.

"OK, Mr. Harkness," said Joe. "Let me ask you again. Where were you when Mr. Wallerman was killed? That was Monday night."

"Like I said before, I don't see how that's any of your business."

"Mr. Harkness," said Ginny, "it is our business because we're trying to determine who killed Mr. Wallerman. Those with solid alibis make it onto our 'no' list, and the others go on our 'maybe' list."

"Guess you'll just have to lump me in with all the other maybes."

"Mr. Harkness, how many guns do you own?" asked Joe.

"Who said I owned any?"

"And how many of those are handguns?" continued Joe.

"If and when you get a warrant, you can come by and look for yourselves."

"Mr. Harkness," said Ginny, "why did you write that letter to Mr. Wallerman?"

"Cuz it was how I felt."

"Why? Did one of his clients commit a crime against you?"

"Nope."

"Then why write a letter like that?" asked Joe.

"To let him know how I felt."

"And why'd you feel that way? And why'd you feel it so strongly?"

"Just did."

Harkness refused to answer all but the most mundane questions. After almost an hour, Joe and Ginny had nothing. He refused having a lawyer present, saying he didn't need one as he hadn't done anything wrong and didn't plan to say anything.

"OK. Enough of this, Detectives. This has gotten to be even more boring than my inventory work. Either arrest me or I'm outta here."

Joe and Ginny said that he was free to leave. They warned Harkness not to leave town without talking with them first, gave him their cards and arranged for a patrol car to drive him back to work.

"Joe, that's my kind of suspect. We need to check if there's any history between him, or one of his relatives, and Wallerman or one of Wallerman's clients."

"Yup. I'd love to nail him for it. But now we need to find some evidence other than him having written that letter."

"At least he admitted to the letter. As a minimum, we don't have to track down the remaining Harris or the other Harkness."

"Every little bit helps."

Back at their desks, Joe and Ginny decided they should quickly work through the newspaper articles to see if any other hot suspects surfaced. Ginny started right in on the articles, while Joe first checked the various databases and files on Harkness.

Fifteen minutes later, Joe reported his findings to Ginny. "No rap sheet, no IRS issues and nothing worse than a few speeding tickets over the years. Dropped out of high school after 10th grade. Not surprised — his letter didn't sound like it was written by a brain surgeon."

"Damn," said Ginny. "I would feel better if he were a hardened criminal with a couple of attempted murder convictions, or at least suspicions."

"Yeah. But when was the last time one of our cases was that easy?"

"True enough. Sadly. Anyhow, Harkness remains our top suspect. At least for now. Oh well, Joe, time for you to join me in whittling down this stack of newspaper articles."

Joe and Ginny began grabbing articles from the pile stacked in the center where their two desks touched. Reading the stories, they made notes of any controversial issues, unsavory-sounding characters or just plain unusual things that caught their eye. For any notes they made, they also wrote down the date and page number of the article, and they put a big asterisk on the photocopy of the article to indicate the section of interest. Those stories with nothing of interest went into one pile and those with something of possible interest formed another pile.

"OK, Ginny, of the ones I've reviewed, I pulled aside three."

"And I got four."

"So, we've got a bunch of letter writers and names from newspaper articles to check out. Not terrible, but enough to keep us busy for a bit."

"Yup, now it's time for the real detective work to start."

"You bet. Good thing there are two top-notch detectives right here," said Joe.

Just then Joe's phone rang. "Hello. This is Detective McFarland with the Jasper Creek Police Department."

"Hello, Detective. This is Jane."

"I'm sorry. Who is this?"

"Jane. Jane Daniels. The intern in the prosecutor's office."

"Oh, yes. Of course. I'm so sorry. Excuse me, Jane, but my mind was someplace else. What's up?"

"I finished the assignment that you and Mr. Porter gave me the other day."

"Great. Good for you. What do you have?"

"I finished sorting all our cases to identify those where Mr. Wallerman was the APA."

"Great. How many are there?"

"I don't know if you'll be surprised, but I sure was. He handled a total of about 700 cases while he worked here."

"Yikes. He was a busy man."

"I discussed it with Mr. Porter. Just to do a sanity check. He said that's in line. He said we average about 175 cases a year for each APA. Of course, the numbers vary quite a bit depending on the specific crimes, the ability of the defense attorneys, the number of cases that get pleaded out and so on. But he wasn't surprised by my 700 number."

"OK. And what about the defendants found guilty and the victims of defendants found not guilty? Which have been, shall we say, out of circulation since soon after the crime until recently?"

"I'm only part way through that part. It's a lot slower than just getting Mr. Wallerman's caseload. I have to search several databases, the Internet, Facebook, and so on for each person. But I wanted to give you an update before the weekend."

"Thank you, Jane. That's very thoughtful. And appreciated. So how far along are you with this second part?"

"I'm almost halfway through. I should be all done by Monday afternoon or evening. Mr. Porter authorized me to come in over the weekend to keep working on this."

"We greatly appreciate your efforts on this, Jane. But

be sure to take at least a few hours for yourself over the weekend."

"Oh, I will. Thanks. I'll call you Monday as soon as I'm done."

"Thanks, Jane. Have a good weekend, best you can."

"Thanks, and the same to you."

Joe hung up and turned to Ginny. He filled her in on the conversation. "I think we've got a winner helping us."

"Great. She's taken a big load off our backs."

"Sure has. But she raised an important question for us."

"What's that?" asked Ginny.

"She's going to be working most of the weekend on our behalf. But what are we doing on our behalf this weekend?"

"Joe, I'm surprised to be suggesting this. But I could go for a weekend doing nothing, just hidden away in your house. I'm drained."

"Me too. OK, that's our plan. And if it's nice Sunday, we can take a few hours' drive into the country."

"You're on. And we also need to hold the next of our 'you, me and the chief' discussions at some point over the weekend. Let's call it a day. Our letter writers will still be here on Monday."

"Deal. And we also want to talk with the two soon-to-be-wealthy ex-wives on Monday. You never know what you can learn from ex-wives."

"True. We shall see."

"That we will. You dying for pizza or Chinese tonight, Ginny?"

"Hmm. Tough call. Let's go with Chinese."

"OK. I'll call in our order and then swing by on the way home."

"See you there in a few. See how convenient it is that you gave me a key?"

"Sure do. See you soon."

Chapter 14

Joe and Ginny spent all of Saturday just hanging out at Joe's house. Ginny scraped together lunch and dinner from whatever frozen foods were in Joe's freezer and leftovers in his refrigerator. These weren't gourmet meals, but both detectives were happy just lounging around, talking and doing nothing. They didn't even have the energy for a supermarket trip. The day ended with a movie on HBO after dinner, and then to sleep.

Sunday morning came around earlier than expected.

"OK, lazybones. Today we have to get outside a little. I'm heading out for some bagels and cream cheese and some sandwiches for lunch. While I'm gone, you're in charge of getting the coffee perking. Then we're heading north toward Lima. Don't know how far we'll get. We'll stop someplace for a picnic lunch. And while we're lying around recovering from lunch, we can have our 'you, me and the chief' talk. Then we'll continue on our journey. At some point, we should be able to find a decent restaurant for dinner."

"Boy, you've really got this day planned out."

"Yup, just think of me as your trustworthy Boy Scout leader."

"I can get to semi-trustworthy Boy Scout leader, but that's about as far as I will go."

"Close enough. OK, time to rise and shine." Joe jumped out of bed and pulled the quilt off Ginny.

"OK, leader. Meet you in the shower."

An hour later, Joe and Ginny were in Joe's car heading north. Whenever possible, Joe chose side roads rather than the highway.

The sky was solid blue and the air was crisp and fresh. Joe and Ginny had the windows open, both wishing that the car was a convertible.

After about an hour and a half, Joe turned and followed a narrow, one-lane, gravel road about three miles to where it dead ended in front of a small pine tree forest.

"OK, we've got our picnic spot," said Joe. "You grab the blanket. I've got the sandwiches and the all-important bottle of wine and two paper cups. And, before you ask, no, I didn't bring a corkscrew. But I did make sure I took a bottle with a twist-off cap."

"Smart man."

Ginny found a smooth, level area in the sun just at the edge of the pine trees and carefully laid out the blanket. In the sun, and with the trees blocking most of the wind, it was surprisingly warm. Joe and Ginny sat down on the blanket, talked for a few minutes, kissed for a few more and then focused on lunch. Joe opened the wine bottle and filled the two paper cups. Following a toast without the typical clink of glasses tapping each other, they dug into their Italian sub sandwiches in between sips of wine.

After lunch, they both lay back on the blanket and got into "the discussion."

Ginny filled Joe in on all the details of the calls she had made to the four police departments.

"Joe, as I told you, I don't feel any better since talking with them."

"I can understand that. It seems in these small departments, with or without a formal policy, situations like ours are basically decided by the chief."

"Yeah. And pretty much totally subjectively. 'Best for employee morale and safety.' Hell, the chief can make that mean whatever he wants."

"Yup. At least in large departments, if there's a problem, one of the people can move to another part of the department. That doesn't work for us. Unless one of us goes back to Patrol or becomes a dispatcher."

"Fat chance of that."

"The other thing is the one department that told me it's worse the longer they keep it a secret from the chief."

"Man, we're in one tough spot."

"Joe, that's where we've been for weeks now. We gotta break out of this."

"Agreed. Seems to me we've got two choices. The first is we continue our sneaking around, being as discreet as possible — even though we're pretty sure that nearly everyone has us figured out. Then we officially respond about our relationship once we're facing more than rumors and guesswork. At that point, one of us would have to leave the department, since there's no way to separate us while we're both detectives. Or we both decide to leave, maybe move somewhere and apply together to join a larger department."

"Joe, we may both decide to leave, but don't count on us both getting detective jobs at a large department. I doubt if many departments would hire two people with an existing relationship. They have enough problems when the relationship begins after they're both working there. Plus, we're both up there in years. And even worse, many departments make you start as a patrol officer. No thanks."

"You're right. Plus even in a large department where we might both be able to work, they'd never let us be partners."

"Yeah. And that's pretty important. Hell, we spend way more than half our waking hours either at work or talking about work. And I want us to keep doing that as partners."

"I agree. Maybe we start our own PI firm. Or open a bed and breakfast."

"Why not think big? How about starting an airline?" asked Ginny with half a smile.

"OK. OK. Back to our choices. Our second option is to sit down and talk with the chief soon, hopefully on one of his better days. Level with him and see where it winds up."

"Also pretty scary. But probably the better of the two options. Like we said, our position might be stronger if we quickly solve the Wallerman case and then talk to him."

"Agreed," said Joe.

"OK then. We continue as is for now, and focus on finding Wallerman's killer."

"Sounds like the right strategy. Or at least the best one from the available lousy choices. What say we adjourn this meeting?"

"OK. The official vote is two to zero. Meeting adjourned."

They folded up the blanket, put the sandwich wrappings and the paper cups into a shopping bag serving as their trash bag, screwed the wine bottle cap back on and got back into the car.

Joe drove north in the general direction of Lima. They stayed on back roads for a while, but eventually got onto Route 75. Just before reaching Lima, they stopped at a lovely old house that had been converted into a farm-to-table restaurant. As it wasn't much past five o'clock, they had no trouble getting a table. After an enjoyable meal, which included finishing their two-thirds empty wine bottle from lunch, they were back on the road to Joe's house.

An hour or so of TV, quick showers and they were soon cuddled together in bed. After an especially intense session of lovemaking, Ginny felt sleep coming on, but wanted to say something about their time together on this special day.

"Joe, thanks for a great day. I really enjoyed it."

"Me too. It must have been the great company we had."

Ginny chuckled softly and snuggled closer. "I'm sure it was. Also, thanks for our talk after lunch. I know we didn't really solve anything, but I feel somewhat better after today. We have to keep trying."

"I agree. That's the deal we made and I'm sticking to it. Luckily, in the meantime, while we keep trying, life ain't that bad."

"Amen to that. Good night, Joe."

"Night. Sleep well."

Chapter 15

Both were awakened by the alarm clock at 6:30.
"Yikes, I thought it was still the middle of the
night."

"Yeah, I'm usually awake when the alarm goes off," said
Joe. "But not this morning. I was still sound asleep."

"Well, like it or not, time to rise and shine," said Ginny
as she jumped out of bed.

Ginny was thankful that she had brought several of
her outfits and some makeup to Joe's weeks ago, thereby
allowing her to avoid having to swing by her apartment
to put on fresh clothes. They both dressed a little nicer
than normal, knowing they'd be going to Wallerman's
funeral.

After a quick breakfast of stale bagels and coffee, they
were on their way to the station, in their separate cars.

Back at their desks, Joe asked, "Besides the funeral,
what's on the schedule for today?"

"We said we'd try to visit the vic's two ex-wives. I'll call
them as soon as it's a more respectable hour. We also have
to follow up with that hardworking intern in the prosecutor's office when she calls us later today."

"Right. And any spare time we have can go to working
through all the letter writers we selected for a more
thorough look. See how many we can eliminate as
possible suspects. A fun day coming up. Besides burying

myself in police and DMV databases, looks like a day of Googling, Facebooking and LinkedIning. Plus, of course, my favorites — hospital and death records."

"Sounds like we won't be bored today. Let's start on our selected letter writers, and I'll call the two ex-wives in an hour or so to schedule meetings with them. Before I dive into the letters, I'm going to run checks on the two wives."

"Good idea. Let me refill my coffee cup and I'm good to go. Want a refill?"

"Sure. Thanks," said Ginny as she handed her almost empty cup to Joe.

Joe returned with two cups of coffee and handed Ginny's back to her. "Here you go."

"Thanks."

"Joe, moving right ahead, why don't you start with the remaining four letters you picked out that were sent to the town council. After I run the checks on the ex-wives, I'll work on the seven newspaper articles we selected so far."

"Deal."

Joe spent the next 45 minutes researching three of the four letters to the town council. The fourth letter was from an anonymous writer and offered little hope of identifying him or her. For the other three, Joe checked the state's DMV files, local, state and federal rap sheets, and death certificates in Ohio and surrounding states. He also looked at Facebook, LinkedIn, and other sites before turning to his favorite tool, Google. He was able to eliminate two of the three writers, one being in his mid-80s and the other being in the hospital at the time of Wallerman's homicide, having broken his pelvic bone when a car ran into him on his bicycle. The third, a Brian Johnston, would merit an in-person get-together.

During this same time, Ginny turned to the newspaper articles. She extracted all the relevant names from the seven stories, most describing harsh questioners and protestors at recent town council meetings. For reasons similar to Joe's, she was able to eliminate six of nine names, leaving three for Joe and her to interview.

"Joe, I'm going to take a break and see if the two ex-wives can see us sometime today."

"Go for it."

Ginny made quick work of this.

"OK. We're set to visit wife number one, on the north side, at 12:30 and number two at 3:00. Number two is east, just outside the town limits."

"Good. Well done."

"In the meantime, let's dig into the writers of the remaining letters to Wallerman. Let's each take five and whoever's done first can grab number 11."

"If I didn't care so much about you, that would be a great reason for me to work slowly."

"Very funny. Here're your five," said Ginny as she handed the top five letters to Joe.

About 45 minutes later, Joe said, "I've only finished checking out three, but we should stop now to head over to the church."

"OK. And by the way, just for the official record, I've finished four. Let's head out."

Joe drove, pulling into a no-parking zone directly across the street. They sat in Joe's car for a few minutes, watching people arrive, greet each other and enter the church.

"Very nice," said Joe.

"What is?"

"I expected the place to be virtually empty. But look at the great turnout. All the government officials and several folks I recognize from the prosecutor's office and the courthouse."

"Yes, and it looks like a big turnout from the legal profession. I guess to pay last respects to one of their own."

"And there's Radner. I wonder if his ex-wives are here."

"If you really care that much, Joe, we can ask them when we meet with them later."

At close to 10 o'clock, Joe and Ginny entered the church and sat in the last row of pews.

It was a short ceremony, with no one getting up to say anything about Wallerman. Few of the mourners joined the short procession of cars to the cemetery either. After a brief burial service, Joe and Ginny said quick hellos to Radner and Collins, as well as the mayor and town council chairman, before returning to Joe's car and driving out of the cemetery.

"Joe, there's a great sushi place I know on the north side. Let's eat there."

"Works for me."

"We have to go to the Northside Clinic. Number one works there as an admissions clerk. She arranged for time off at 12:30. We can sit with her in the cafeteria."

"Then I definitely want to get sushi. Hospital cafeterias are pretty close to the bottom of my list."

"Gotcha."

"Ginny, we did the right thing, but, as expected, we saw nothing or no one unusual at the funeral."

"Yeah, but you never know in advance."

"True enough."

They arrived at the sushi restaurant a few minutes later.

Chapter 16

After an enjoyable lunch, Joe drove to the clinic and parked out front. They walked in, showed their badges and were told how to get to the cafeteria, located in the basement.

Walking into the depressing, faded yellow cafeteria, Ginny immediately noticed one woman sitting by herself in the back corner, with a bowl of soup in front of her.

Ginny walked over. "Ms. Baines?"

"Yes. Are you Detective . . .? Um, I'm sorry. The detective who called me this morning?"

"Yes. I'm Detective Harris. And that's my partner, Detective McFarland, waiting over there. Let us get a couple of cups of coffee and we'll join you. Would you like a cup?"

"No, thanks. I've got my soup."

Joe bought two cups of coffee. He and Ginny each carried a cup. They sat down, one on each side of Baines.

Taking a small sip of the very hot coffee, Ginny asked, "Ms. Baines, I noticed you at the funeral this morning."

"Yes, I was at the church service. But I didn't go to the cemetery. I had to get to work."

"As I mentioned over the phone," said Ginny, "we're investigating the death of Mr. Wallerman and hoped that you might be able to help us."

"I'm happy to try. But, as I told you when you called, I doubt if I can be of any help. Carl and I got divorced more than 20 years ago. Other than running into him around town once every few years, we've not been in touch since then. We had no children. It was an amicable divorce, and he only paid me alimony for about three years. It ended when I remarried."

"Ms. Baines, would you mind telling us why you got divorced?"

"Sure. We were only married a little over four years. Turned out that he was so committed to his job in the prosecutor's office he had no time for anything else. Including me. And my desire to have children before I got too old. Happily, I'm now remarried and have two wonderful children, a boy and a girl, both in their teens."

"I'm glad for you, Ms. Baines," said Ginny.

"Any idea at all who would want to kill Mr. Wallerman?" asked Joe.

"No one specific, but I'd guess it was one of those bums he hung out with."

"Can you be more specific?"

"Well, when we were married and he was an assistant prosecuting attorney, he was always meeting with all kinds of criminal types, sometimes even in our house, who he worked with as witnesses and informants in cases he was prosecuting. And although we were divorced by then, I can only imagine it got even worse when he starting defending them all. When you're dealing with that class of people, something like this shouldn't be so surprising, if you know what I mean."

"Yes, we do," said Ginny. "When was the last time you saw Mr. Wallerman?"

"Not sure. It's been at least a couple of years since we bumped into each other."

"Just for the record, can you tell us where you were last Monday evening, that's the 23rd, when Mr. Wallerman was killed?"

"Wow. You don't mess around. Am I a suspect?"

"No, Ms. Baines. Detective McFarland asked as part of our routine. The more people we can definitively eliminate as possible suspects, the more progress we can make."

"Well, I should be in pretty good shape then. I was here that evening in a training session. We're installing a new computer system, and we all have to get trained on it. Plenty of people saw me here. Training went from seven to 10, then a group of us went out for a few drinks. I didn't get home until a little after 11:30. I remember because I was exhausted the next day."

At Ginny's request, Baines took Ginny's notepad and wrote the names of a few of her colleagues who could confirm her alibi.

Retrieving her notepad and pen, Ginny said, "Well, thank you for your time. Here's my card. Please call me if you think of anything that might be of interest to us."

"OK," said Baines as she took the card.

"Thank you for your time," said Joe as he and Ginny stood.

"You're welcome. And good luck with your investigation."

Ten minutes later, after a stop in the restrooms on the way out, Joe and Ginny were in the car heading to ex-wife number two.

"Well, that was a waste," said Ginny. "I'll check her alibi with the names she wrote down, just to be sure."

"Yeah. I'm not surprised. They've been divorced and basically out of touch for 20 years. But we had to give it a shot."

"Right. Seemed like a pleasant woman. Glad she got the kids she wanted."

"Are you telling me something?"

"No. Just saying. She wanted them and she got them. End of story."

"And what about you? Ever think about kids? Sorry you don't have any?"

"I don't know. I do and I don't. I miss not bringing up a kid. But I love my freedom. I'm sure I'll regret it to some degree when I'm old and gray without any kids or grand-kids."

"You're only 35. You can still do it if you want."

"I know. We'll see. Let's get you and me figured out first."

"Fair enough. What's the address for number two?"

Ginny checked her notepad. "1684 East Sunset. Building G. It's a trailer park on the right about two miles past the town line. Called Vista Estates."

"Got it. Vista Estates. Sounds pretty fancy. But it is a trailer park. Should be there in 20 or 25 minutes."

Sure enough, 25 minutes later Joe entered the Vista Estates entrance and pulled up in front of the trailer marked "Building G."

"Well. I am impressed," said Joe. "When you said it was a trailer park, I wasn't sure what to expect. But this is really pretty pleasant. The flowers and everything. Nicely kept up. And a decent amount of space between the trailers."

"Yeah. And most of the trailers look to be in good shape. We're early, but let's go see if number two is there."

Joe and Ginny got out, walked up the three brick steps and knocked on the door.

"Coming. One minute please."

Less than a minute later, the door opened. "Hi. I'm Louise Landell. You must be the detectives."

"Yes, that's correct, Ms. Landell. I'm Detective Harris and this is Detective McFarland."

"Come in," said Landell as she opened the door wider.

Joe and Ginny followed her in and, at her suggestion, took seats in the small living room or sitting area.

"I know you want to talk about Carl. Do you know who killed him? Or why? Man, they sure screwed me big time."

"No. We don't know yet. But we're working on it. Why do you say they screwed you?" asked Joe.

"Dead men don't pay alimony."

"Was Mr. Wallerman paying you alimony? And will that now stop?" asked Ginny.

"Yes to both those questions. I don't know what I'm going to do. I haven't been able to find work, especially because I don't have a car. Those alimony payments were the only thing between me and the poorhouse."

"Sorry to hear that," said Joe. "How much longer were the payments scheduled to go for?"

"'Til he hit 65. Unless I remarried. Fat chance of that. Or, as it turns out, unless he dies."

"When was the last time you saw Mr. Wallerman?"

"Not sure. Probably three or four years ago. We don't exactly travel in the same social circles. But I have to admit, he was a man of his word. I got that alimony payment in my bank right on time every month."

"Any idea who might have wanted him dead?"

"Probably one of his lousy clients. I'm sure almost all of them were guilty. But he really believed that crap about everyone deserving a good lawyer. Even the guilty. And, let me tell you, a lot of them were guilty of being evil."

"Any specific ones come to mind who you think we should look into?"

"All of them."

"Can we ask why you two got divorced?"

"It was them. I kept bad-mouthing his clients and he kept defending them. Pretty soon it went from that to us disagreeing and fighting about almost everything."

"Anything else you can tell us to help us solve the case?"

"No. Sorry, I can't think of anything else."

"Ms. Landell," said Joe. "I didn't notice you at Mr. Wallerman's funeral this morning. Were you there?"

"No. It's difficult without a car. Plus, I haven't seen Carl in years. When he was alive. Surely no need to see him when he's dead."

"I understand," said Joe. "Just for the record, can you tell us where you were last Monday evening, which is when Mr. Wallerman was killed?"

"Easy. Since that was a weekday, almost for sure, I was right here. Either watching TV or sleeping."

"Ms. Landell," said Ginny, "was anyone here with you who can confirm that?"

"Afraid not. Although I've got a few friends here, we don't do much evening socializing, except for sometimes on the weekends."

"Ok, that's it for now. We may be back if we have any additional questions," said Ginny as she gave a business card to Landell. Ginny and Joe said their goodbyes and left.

Back in the car heading into town, Ginny said, "Wife number one sure has a better alibi than number two."

"Yeah. But I actually feel bad for number two. Seems like she got totally dependent on the alimony, and probably welfare payments, and now just had the rug pulled out from under her. Unless, of course, she knew about his will and is the perp."

"Yeah. I agree. I would have referred her to social services, except for the hefty inheritance she's about to receive."

"That's a pretty nice motive. Upwards of half of a mil," said Joe. "The key is when she knew about it."

"Right you are. And, like we said, she clearly doesn't have much of an alibi."

"Well, her luck and financial situation will really change when she gets her 25 percent."

"Very true. Think it's too late for me or you to get on that 25 percent list?"

"Joe!"

"Just kidding. But it sure would be nice."

When they got back to their desks, there was a phone message for Joe. Jane Daniels from the prosecutor's office had called and left a message. She'd finished her assignment, but had to leave early, to the dentist with a tooth-ache. Joe should call her in the morning.

Joe and Ginny straightened out the papers on their desks and called it a day. They decided to each go to their own house that night to do some house cleaning and get a good night's sleep.

Chapter 17

Back at their desks the next morning, Ginny said, "OK. Time to get to work. Let's see if we can whittle down our list of possible suspects. And at some point this morning, you need to call that prosecutor intern."

"I know. I was also thinking we should head out to the vic's house and talk with his neighbors." Before Ginny could respond, Joe continued, "The uniforms canvassed the whole area and learned nada. But they were asking about the homicide. We need to get a better handle on his lifestyle. Was he out a lot? Wild parties? Coming home with different women or always the same one? Or men? That kind of thing."

"Good idea. Let's save that for late in the day. We'll have a better chance of catching more of them home close to dinner time."

"You're right. Let me get a cup of coffee and a refill for you. Then we'll be ready to dive in."

Joe returned a couple of minutes later, gave Ginny her refilled coffee cup and sat down at his desk.

"OK, Joe. Let's first finish the 11 letters to Wallerman that we started on yesterday."

"Roger that."

They both started researching the few letters they hadn't got to the day before.

Joe took a short break around 9:15. He called Jane

Daniels, the intern in the prosecutor's office, and arranged to visit her at 11 o'clock.

About 10:15, Ginny and Joe finished the remainder of the hate letters to Wallerman.

"OK, Ginny. Whatcha got?"

"I eliminated three of the six I took. Of the three meriting follow-up, one is unsigned so there's only two for follow-up right now."

"Good. I also have three."

"By the way, Joe, the Gould letter that matched one of the Wallerman letters was not one of the Wallerman letters we picked for initial follow-up."

"Naturally," said Joe as he raised his eyebrows and looked to the sky. "Why should anything be too easy for us with this case?"

"Well, we can start with the ones where we do have names, and even addresses. But first we should mosey over to the prosecutor's office."

"Right."

A few minutes later and Joe and Ginny were squeezed into her work cubicle with Daniels.

Joe introduced her and Ginny to each other, and then said, "Jane, how's your tooth? Not much I hate more than a toothache and the dentist."

"He really helped me. And with enough lidocaine, I didn't mind the drilling."

"OK, enough. My teeth are starting to hurt just listening to you."

"Jane," said Ginny, "the message you left for Joe yesterday said that you were finished. We're anxious to see what you found."

"Yes, of course. I'm sorry. Here's a printout of what I came up with, but let me walk you through it," said Daniels as she handed Ginny a three-page computer printout. "I'm sort of finished. You'll see what I mean in a minute."

"OK. Start walking," said Joe.

"Will do. During Mr. Wallerman's five years here, he worked on 1,042 cases. This includes those approximately 700 where he was first chair, plus those where he was second chair. Of these, the defendant was found guilty or pleaded guilty 768 times. Of these guilty ones, only 23 saw the defendant released from prison in the past 18 months. All the others were either released earlier than that, are still in prison or died in prison. Then, using various other databases, I reduced the 23 to nine. The others were in the hospital or overseas or at a very public event far from here at the time of the murder. Where I could find it, I included the last-known address for each of these nine."

"That's great work, Jane," said Ginny.

"Yes, it is," added Joe.

"Thanks," said Daniels.

"Jane," asked Joe, "where are you with the not-guilty group?"

"That's where you won't be as happy. I split the 274 not-guilty cases into two groups — those related to serious injury or death to someone in one group and all the other less serious crimes in the other. There were 17 serious crimes and 257 less serious ones."

"Good," said Joe. "So where are you with the 17?"

"No place. To really examine these, we need to list the

actual victim plus family members and good friends. This is a big job just to get all the names. Then I'd first have to check for all of these people whether they're still alive and healthy, were somehow not available to kill Mr. Wallerman until now and so on. And yesterday afternoon, when Mr. Porter asked me for a status report, he said I should leave this for you to do. That I had to get back to doing work he had for me. Sorry."

"No need to apologize, Jane," said Ginny. "You've done a great job and helped us a lot."

"Yes, you definitely have. Jane, one important question. Is there a Paul Harkness on any of your lists?"

"Is that H-A-R-K-N-E-S-S?"

"Yes, that's right."

"Give me a minute to check."

"Sure," said Ginny. "Take your time."

Then, a minute later, "No. I'm sorry. No Paul Harkness."

"Too bad," said Joe. "But it was worth a shot."

"But there is a Martha Harkness."

"Oh. Tell us more," said Ginny.

"OK. Give me a minute. I need the case number to pull up the file."

Then a minute later, "Here it is."

Joe and Ginny crowded around Jane's computer monitor. It turned out that Martha Harkness was raped by one of the defendants whom Wallerman unsuccessfully prosecuted several years ago. A few more minutes and Jane was able to identify Martha as the daughter of Paul Harkness. Martha had been living in southern California, where she committed suicide a few months earlier.

"Very sad," said Joe. "But now we have a nice juicy motive for Paul Harkness."

"I bet we've got enough for a search warrant or two," said Ginny.

"You bet. Let's check with Porter while we're here." Then turning to Jane, Joe continued, "Jane, we're heading out for lunch after we speak with Mr. Porter. Would you like to join us?"

"Thank you. But I think I'll pass. I wasn't sure how my tooth would be today, so I brought a salad from home."

"OK. We'll give you a raincheck. And, again, thanks for all your help."

"You're very welcome. I actually enjoyed the work. Bye for now."

Joe and Ginny said their goodbyes and walked over to Porter's office.

"Charles, have a couple of minutes?" asked Ginny.

"Sure. Come on in."

Joe and Ginny walked into Porter's office and took the two seats in front of his desk.

"Charles," said Joe. "Jane was really helpful with her computer stuff. As you know, she didn't finish everything, but she made a lot of progress. Thanks for the help."

"Welcome."

"Charles," said Ginny. "Based on a threatening letter that he wrote to Mr. Wallerman, coupled with Jane helping us learn that his daughter, who just recently committed suicide, had been raped by a suspect whom Wallerman was unsuccessful in prosecuting, we think we have a very viable suspect. And he couldn't or wouldn't provide an alibi."

"Good work. Sounds like a hot lead."

"It is," said Joe. "Which is why we'd like a search warrant for his house and where he works. Plus a subpoena to have his cellphone provider give us his locations the night of the homicide."

"Should be doable. You've got that letter, no alibi and a plausible motive. Give me a few hours. I'll call you when I have something."

Joe and Ginny gave Porter Harkness' full name, his address, and the address of his employer. They thanked Porter and left. Without even discussing it, they walked directly to Sancho's Taco Shop and were soon eating their customary lunch.

As they finished eating, Ginny said, "OK. Back to work. We've got a lot of following up to do. Thirteen people including two anonymous folks from the letters and newspaper work we did, plus Jane's list of nine guilty defendants and 17 not-guilty defendants of serious crimes. Plus who knows how many family members and friends. And for now, Harkness remains at the top of our suspect list and that Johnston fellow is at the top of our to-visit list."

"We better get started. Plus, don't forget, later today we want to take a run at the neighbors."

"I know. I didn't forget."

"It'd be nice if we got those Harkness search warrants today. I know that the cellphone tracking will take a few days to get. Jane was a big help. It would have taken us at least twice as long to do what she did. When it comes to computer work, the younger the better. They grew up with computers and smart phones and all that stuff.

What you and I have to carefully think out, it's just second nature to them."

"Speak for yourself, Grandpa."

"So if you're not Grandma, do you want to be my daughter or granddaughter?"

"How about just your young and beautiful girlfriend? Maybe even your trophy girlfriend," said Ginny as she chuckled.

"Works for me."

Joe and Ginny paid for their lunches, walked back to the station, filled their coffee cups and sat down at their desks.

"OK, Joe. We've run out of shortcuts. We gotta go through the list we have, one by one, and see who can be eliminated, or at least put at the bottom of our list, and who can't."

"Yeah. And all this assumes the perp is this easily identified. It just as likely could have been someone who didn't write a letter first or wasn't mentioned in a newspaper article about the vic."

"I'm well aware of that. Plus, as we said earlier, the homicide could be totally unrelated to the vic's legal or town council work."

"Sad but true."

"Well, let's start with what we have. We can always expand the pool if we have to."

"OK. But before we jump in, we're overdue on bringing the chief up to date."

"You're right. Out of character for you to think of something like that."

"Well, I want us to stay on his good side. In case we have the big discussion with him."

"Good thinking."

Joe and Ginny walked down to the chief's office and gave him a five-minute summary of where they were. And weren't.

"Appreciate the update, guys. But I'd rather hear about progress than all your hard work."

"Understood, Chief," said Joe. "But we won't get progress without a lot of work."

"Goes without saying. But we're into week two," said the chief as he held up his right hand with his index and middle fingers extended. "All you've got so far are a bunch of possible motives and a long list of possible suspects to chase down for just two of those possible motives."

"I think I've mentioned it before. We're cops, not magicians. Plus, we do have a couple of specific leads to follow up on. That fellow Harkness just might be good for the murder. And we still need to interview that other letter writer, Johnston."

"Yeah, I know, Joe. Just blowing off steam. Everyone and his uncle, from the mayor to the town council chairman to the prosecutor to the press, are all over me on this. But I shouldn't be passing the shit down the line."

"Not a problem, Chief. We understand," said Ginny.

"And we are doing all we can," added Joe. "We greatly reduced the number of angry letter writers to follow up on. And we're going back to the vic's neighborhood later today to try to get a handle on some of his girlfriends. Or dates. Or whatever the hell they were."

"Good. Keep at it. Something'll develop. You two have my full support."

"Thanks, Chief. That means a lot," said Ginny.

"Yeah," mumbled Joe.

Chapter 18

Soon back at their desks, Joe called the home of Brian Johnston, the fellow who had written to the town council. He spoke with his wife and found out that he worked as a security guard at one of the three grade schools in town. Joe and Ginny drove to the school, went to the office and asked to speak with Johnston. A few minutes later, a very tall, very overweight man entered the office. He was wearing a private security firm outfit, with the pants and belt pulled tight under his bulging belly and the buttons on his shirt looking like they were just about ready to pop.

"Someone looking for me?"

"Yes, those folks over there, Mr. Johnston. They're from the police," said the receptionist as she pointed to Joe and Ginny standing at one end of the counter.

"Why not? It's been that kind of day." Turning toward Joe and Ginny, he asked, "You looking for me?"

"Yes, we are," answered Joe. "If you're Brian Johnston."

"Well, that's who I am. What's this about?"

"Is there a place we can sit down and talk for a few minutes?"

Johnston looked at the receptionist, who said, "The conference room is empty now. You can use it."

"OK," said Johnston as he led the detectives next door into the conference room.

Joe introduced himself and Ginny, and all three sat down at the table.

"So?"

"Mr. Johnston, we want to talk to you about the letter you wrote to the town council a couple of months ago."

"What about it?"

"You seemed to be quite upset about the council considering having the town become a sanctuary for illegal immigrants."

"Damn right."

"Can you explain that a little more?" asked Ginny.

"Ain't much to explain. We shouldn't be protecting people who break the law. We have laws for a reason. The town council can't pick and choose which federal laws to obey."

"Mr. Johnston," said Joe, "how strongly do you feel about that?"

"Very strongly. I'd do all I can to not let that happen."

"Even so far as to kill one of the council members proposing that resolution?"

"Whoa. Hold on. Now I see where you're going with this. You think that 'cause I wrote that letter that I killed that councilman, whatever his name is."

"Did you?" asked Joe.

"No way. You can check my record. And you can talk to people. I ain't never done nothing like that. I might get mad and yell and scream, but that's about it."

"Mr. Johnston," asked Ginny, "where were you Monday evening of last week?"

"Same place as always on Mondays. Home with the

wife and kids. We go to bed early. The kids need to leave early for school and I need to be here by 7 o'clock."

"Can anyone except your wife and children confirm that you were home that evening?"

"Of course not. It's our house, not a hotel. Who else do you think would be there?"

"OK," said Joe. "What time did you get home that day? And what time did you go to sleep?"

"Again, like always on weekdays. I was home by five o'clock and we were all in bed by a few minutes after nine. And, no, no one except my wife was in bed with me to prove it."

"Do you think anyone saw you come home that evening? Like a neighbor?" asked Joe.

"No idea. But even if they did, they probably don't remember because it was like all the other nights."

"How many handguns do you own, Mr. Johnston?" asked Ginny.

"What?" I don't own any. I got little kids at home. Think I'm crazy?"

"No, sir," answered Ginny. "We're just trying to be thorough with everyone we talk with."

"Uh. OK."

"Mr. Johnston, that's it for now. We'll be in touch if we have any more questions," said Ginny.

With that, they all got up and left the conference room. Johnston turned left down a long hallway. Joe and Ginny turned right, left the building and got back into Joe's car.

"He seemed believable," said Ginny.

"I agree. No real alibi, but I felt like he was telling the truth. I say he goes to the bottom of our list. But I do want to check if he has a rap sheet. Or if he's on one of Jane's lists."

"Agreed. While we're in the area, let's catch that other letter writer who lives nearby. Hold on, let me dig out his address." Then after rummaging through her folder, "Here it is. He's over on 14th. Take a left at the corner."

Joe drove there. As soon as a nurse answered the door and Joe and Ginny learned that the letter writer had been bedridden for almost two weeks with pneumonia, they knew they had one less possible suspect. Just to be sure, Ginny got the name of his doctor. Joe and Ginny then made a hasty retreat.

Back in the car, Joe said, "Well, that was an easy one. We can cross him off the list once the doctor confirms he was bedridden the day of the killing."

"No question."

Back at the station, Ginny called the doctor to obtain the dates of pneumonia and treatment. The doctor confirmed that the patient had been released from the hospital the day before the murder, and was surely bedridden at home for at least three days after that. Ginny then also called the colleagues that Wallerman's first wife had given to her. Ginny reached two of the three, and both confirmed that Baines had been with them at the computer training session that evening, after which a group of them went out for a few drinks.

While Ginny was checking the alibis, Joe checked for a rap sheet for Brian Johnston. He also checked whether he was on any of the lists developed by Jane. No to both.

Two of the names from the newspaper articles were quickly and easily eliminated. One's Facebook account had pictures of him and his wife and three other couples on vacation in Cancun. Fortunately, the other couples were named. Ginny was able to get the phone numbers and called two of the other wives, both of whom confirmed the trip and its dates.

The other possible suspect had an equally good alibi. He was in Chicago on business Monday morning through Wednesday evening. This was confirmed to Joe by a colleague who traveled with the possible suspect and by two customers whom they called on in Chicago.

"OK, Joe. Enough of this for today. We made some decent progress."

"Yeah, we did. Especially if we don't think about all the names that Jane got us from the prosecutor's files. In any event, I still have that Harkness guy in my sights."

"Agreed. Let's head out now and talk to some of Wallerman's neighbors. It's close to dinner time. Hopefully we'll catch a few at home."

"Sounds good to me. Why don't you drop your car off at my place on the way? Then we can go in my car. And maybe even grab a bite to eat afterwards."

"You mean in plain, local sight? Where we might be seen?"

"Yeah. We worked late to catch the vic's neighbors at home, and then grabbed dinner. A nice, acceptable, and conveniently true explanation."

"Works for me. I love the idea of not having to drive an hour away for dinner so no one sees us."

"Me too. This is our lucky day."

"OK. I'm heading out in five. See you at your place."

"That's a date, Partner."

Chapter 19

Joe left about 10 minutes after Ginny. She was in her car across the street from his house when he got home. Joe opened his garage with the remote in his car and Ginny drove in. Two minutes later, they were both in Joe's car on the way to Wallerman's neighborhood.

"I've got a second remote for the garage door someplace in the house. Gotta dig it out for you so you don't have to park out front when I'm not there."

"Much appreciated."

Joe and Ginny were soon parked in front of Wallerman's house. The crime scene tape was still attached to the trees out front. To double their efficiency, they decided to split up. Joe went left and Ginny went right.

Ginny rang the doorbell at the house next to Wallerman's. When no one answered, she knocked on the door. Still no answer. She got luckier at the house across the street.

The door was opened by an attractive, brown-haired woman in her early 40s. "Yes, can I help you?"

"Good evening, I'm Detective Harris with the Jasper Creek Police Department."

"Oh, my God! What happened? Is it my husband? My son?"

"No ma'am. Sorry to have frightened you. We're investigating the recent death of Mr. Wallerman across the street, and I'd like to ask you a few questions."

"Whew! You scared me half to death. My husband and son are running a few errands before dinner. I thought something happened to them. But, uh yes, sure you can ask me whatever you want about poor Carl. What a shame. Come in, please. Oh, and I'm so sorry, I didn't even introduce myself. I'm Roberta England."

"Thank you," said Ginny as she followed England into her front parlor, where they both sat down."

"Ms. England, were you or any of your family members home Monday evening last week, when Mr. Wallerman was killed?"

"Yes, we all were. We almost always have dinner at home during the week. Then we watch some TV while Eric does his homework. And we're usually in bed after the nine o'clock news."

"Do you remember seeing or hearing anything unusual that evening?"

"No. Nothing. I remember talking about it the next evening. We didn't learn about it until then because we were gone, my husband and me to work and Eric to school, before all the excitement with the police and all on Tuesday morning. Tuesday evening we saw the police tape and stuff and got the whole story from the neighbors. And then from the six o'clock news. Needless to say, this is still the main topic of conversation around here."

"Yes, I can imagine it is. Ms. England, how well did you know Mr. Wallerman?"

"Um, I'd call us friendly neighbors. But not really friends. We'd wave when we drove past each other, or chat for a few minutes when we were both outside working on the lawn or getting the mail."

"How long did you know him?"

"About five years. That's when we moved here. Carl was already living here. But he was already divorced so our lifestyles were rather different."

"In what way?"

"Well, we basically did stuff as a family, or sometimes just husband and wife if Eric didn't join us. But Carl was either alone or with one of his flings."

"His flings?"

"Oh. I really shouldn't have said that. But that's what we called them. He pretty much had a steady stream of young, pretty guests. And they often spent the whole night or even a few nights in a row with him. Not that I'm judging. I know how things have changed these days."

"Do you know the names of any of these women? Or would you recognize them if you saw them again?"

"Definitely no on the names. We never knew their names or met any of them. Carl would park in his driveway or garage, and we'd see him and his visitor get out of the car in the driveway or in the garage before the garage door closed. I don't think Carl was really trying to hide them. I mean, he was single, you know. But he didn't want to advertise their presence either. If you know what I mean."

"Yes, I do. Were any of these women what you might call a regular, or were they always different?"

"Hard to say. You could sometimes notice the color of their hair or their body shape, but that was about it. Especially since it was often dark or getting dark when they arrived. There definitely were several different women, but who knows how many came here how many times."

"Did any of these women drive here in their own cars?"

"Not that we ever saw. It's possible that some did, but we didn't see or at least we didn't notice it. It was like he was happy for people to see that he could attract pretty, young women, but he didn't want people to recognize or get to know who the women were. Maybe they were married women, for all I know."

"Do you know that for a fact or are you just saying maybe?"

"Oh, just saying maybe. We really don't know. But it's interesting. Carl, bless his soul, was reasonably handsome, and he was not a bad physical specimen, if you know what I mean. And, I'm sure you know, some women fall for older, successful and so-called powerful men. I mean, look at the women that used to hang around Henry Kissinger's feet. Kissinger clearly isn't what you'd call a hunk. Carl wasn't any Henry Kissinger, but in little Jasper Creek he was on the town council and was a big, successful lawyer."

"Can you think of anyone who had a disagreement with him? Or might want to kill him?"

"No. But, like I said before, we didn't really know him well."

"OK, then. Thank you for your time. Here's one of my cards. Please call me if you think of anything else or if your husband or son can add anything to what we discussed."

"I sure will."

After a quick goodbye, Ginny was back on the street.

Ginny tried about 10 more houses on the street, and was able to talk with someone at seven of them. Most knew about the same as or less than England did. No one seemed to be really friendly with Wallerman, but no one had any problems with him. Almost all knew about his bringing several different women home, but no one knew anything that Ginny hadn't learned from her talk with England.

Joe had similar results as he canvassed his half of the block. No one knew Wallerman well; most knew he brought a stream of young, attractive women home, but that was about it.

Ginny and Joe met back at Joe's car almost two hours later. They were tired and it was getting dark.

Joe told Ginny that Porter had called him about 20 minutes earlier. He had gotten the warrants and subpoena regarding Harkness. He faxed the warrants to Joe and Ginny and the subpoena to Harkness' cellphone provider. Given the late hour, Joe and Ginny decided to pursue the warrants first thing in the morning. Joe called the Patrol Division and requested two officers to help with the search the next morning. He asked that the officers pick up the warrants sitting on the fax machine near Joe's desk and bring them with them to Harkness' house at seven the next morning.

"OK, that's done. Let's get going," said Joe. "I'm starved. We can compare notes over dinner."

"Sounds good to me. Where we gonna eat?"

"Any preferences?"

"No. Other than something different than tacos, pizza or Chinese."

"Oh, you really want to go exotic, do you?"

"Depends on what you call exotic. Exotic to me is something like alligator tail. Or lion steak."

"Well, let's not go that exotic. How about a good old plain beef steak? Gerald's is only about a mile from here. I've not eaten there, but I've heard good things."

"Let's do it, Joe. I'm sure we don't need a reservation on a Tuesday night."

Joe took the next two rights, made a left turn after about a half mile and was soon in front of Gerald's. He parked in the street a half block away, and he and Ginny walked to the restaurant. Almost half the tables were empty, and they were seated immediately.

After reviewing the menu, Joe ordered a shrimp cocktail and sirloin steak for himself, plus a loaded baked potato and creamed spinach for Ginny and him to share. Ginny went with a house salad and a filet mignon. Joe then selected a bottle of a California cabernet sauvignon.

While eating and drinking, they talked about their questioning of Wallerman's neighbors. They both referred to their notes several times to be sure not to miss or misstate anything.

"That's about it," said Joe. "Like you, I left my card with everyone I talked with, but I don't expect a flood of calls. In fact, I don't even expect one."

"Yeah. He seemed to be rather private. Cordial, but not one to mix with his neighbors. As several said, a friendly neighbor but not a friend."

"Maybe he was too busy with all his young girlfriends to make friends with the neighbors."

"Joe, you sound jealous," said Ginny with a smile.

"No, just observing. I'm more than happy with just the one young, pretty girl I've got."

"How sweet, Joe."

"There is one important lesson, though."

"What's that?"

"We think we're so careful and sneaky when you come to my house. And we hide your car in the garage. Well, if my neighbors are even half as alert as Wallerman's, we're not fooling anyone. And probably the same when I come to your place."

"Yikes. You're probably right. But I'm not really concerned about your or my neighbors knowing, except that the more people who know, the bigger the risk of it getting back to the chief."

"Yup. Which is why we gotta figure out what we're going to do sooner rather than later."

"Full agreement on that. But back to our interviews, Joe. There is one other conclusion to draw."

"What's that?"

"In addition to his law career and his town council work, the motive could be related to one of these women. One of them he stopped seeing. Or the angry husband or boyfriend of one of them."

"Thanks, Ginny. Just what we need. More unidentified possible perps. We're supposed to be narrowing down the suspect pool, not enlarging it."

"What can I tell you?"

"I know. Just kidding. You're right, of course. But this sure doesn't reduce our workload."

"Can't argue with that. And to make things even worse, we haven't yet heard back from Wallerman's paralegal.

She promised to call by now. God knows how many additional names she's got for us from their files."

"A bunch, I bet. Despite us not suffering from a lack of names, I'll call her tomorrow."

"Good. At the same time, we should go through Wallerman's calendar. Maybe some of his so-called flings are on it."

"OK. That's for tomorrow."

Chapter 20

Joe and Ginny drove to Harkness' apartment very early after meeting in the station's parking lot, where they left Joe's car. By 6:40, they were parked in front of Harkness' apartment building, waiting for the arrival of the two uniformed officers coming to help with the search and bringing the search warrants with them. The officers arrived a few minutes before seven, and Joe and Ginny led them to Harkness' apartment.

Harkness answered the door in his pajamas and a robe. The jam next to his mouth was strong evidence that he was among those who ate breakfast before shaving, showering and dressing for work. After a few minutes of heated discussion, Harkness scanned the search warrant handed to him and reluctantly let the officers proceed with their search. Their discussion had been loud enough that Harkness' wife had been awakened and soon joined the group, she in a nightgown and robe.

The search of the small, one-bedroom apartment, as well as the garage and storage space assigned to Harkness' apartment, uncovered nothing of interest: no gun, no incriminating documents, nothing. Harkness then dressed and followed Joe and Ginny to Jasper Electronics. A search of his locker also turned up nothing.

"Hope you're satisfied now. Maybe you can stop harassing me for a while."

"Mr. Harkness," said Ginny, "we're not trying to harass you. We're just doing our job. We're investigating a murder, you know."

"Yes, I do know that. In any event, it sure as hell feels like harassment."

"Well, sorry about that. We do have a couple of additional questions."

"Why aren't I surprised? What?"

"Tell us about your daughter. Martha, I believe."

"What about her?"

"We understand she recently committed suicide. Our sincere condolences," said Ginny.

"Yeah. Thanks. She was living in California. My wife and I just got back from there a few weeks ago."

"What was your daughter's involvement with Mr. Wallerman?" asked Joe.

"He was the one who prosecuted the bastard who raped her years ago. Poor Martha, she was never the same after that. Afraid of her shadow, almost never leaving her apartment except to go to work or the supermarket. Moved to California, hoping he couldn't ever find her again. And the bastard was found not guilty. Don't know where that Wallerman bought his law degree from, but no matter how cheap it was, he overpaid. He sure failed miserably as a prosecutor."

"Any chance that your daughter's suicide led you to kill Mr. Wallerman?"

"I thought about it. And would have loved to. But, no, I didn't do it. Didn't have the balls to carry it through. Not even for my daughter. Some father!"

"Mr. Harkness, it's good that you didn't," said Ginny.

"Spending the rest of your life in jail now wouldn't do anything to help your daughter. Or your wife."

"Yeah, I know. But, still . . . ."

"Want to tell us where you were the night of the murder yet?" asked Joe.

"No."

"Suit yourself, but it isn't making it easier for us to eliminate you as a suspect."

"Yeah, well it's not my mission in life to make your jobs easier for you."

"OK. Mr. Harkness, thank you for your cooperation this morning. And again, we're sorry about your daughter."

"Yeah."

Joe and Ginny were back in the car, heading for the station.

"Bummer," said Joe. "I was hoping we'd find the smoking gun."

"Me too. But we both knew the odds of that happening."

"Jeez, we should hit the lottery once in a while."

"I'd be all for that. But we did confirm what could be one helluva strong motive."

"That's true."

Joe and Ginny were back at their desks a little after nine. Shortly after they sat down, the chief called them to his office.

"I trust no major breakthrough yet."

"Progress, but no great breakthrough," said Joe.

"So to summarize, you've spent a helluva lot of time working very hard on this. And we still have dozens of suspects, several of whom we don't even have a name or description for. We don't even know what the motive was. Was it related to his legal work, or the town council, or his sex life or who knows what? Have I summarized it correctly?"

'Fraid so. But you make it sound desperate when you put it that way," said Joe.

"Just callin' 'em like I see 'em."

"OK, though we do have that letter writer, Harkness, as a prime suspect," interjected Ginny. "We searched his apartment and workplace this morning. Found nothing, but he still looks promising to us. Hell of a strong motive. And apparently no alibi. We're waiting on a location-history dump from his cellphone."

"OK, good. Keep me up to date. And do me two favors."

"Shoot," said Joe.

"Bring our friendly prosecutor up to speed. He called twice yesterday. I'd rather not talk to him until we have some real progress."

"OK," said Ginny. "We will. And the second favor?"

Staring first at Joe and then at Ginny, the chief said, "Solve this damn thing. And fast."

"We're trying," said Joe.

"I know. I know. Keep at it and good luck."

"Thanks, Chief," said Ginny as she and Joe left the chief's office and returned to their desks.

"Well, I knew that wouldn't be a pleasant discussion. And I wasn't surprised," said Joe.

"Yeah, well I'm sure he's getting a lot of heat from upstairs."

"I know. But we don't need to be kicked in the pants. We're doing all we can. And as fast as we can."

"Yes, we are. OK, I'm going to call Porter to schedule a meeting for later today so we can get another kick in the pants. From him this time."

"Great. My butt and I can't wait," said Joe.

Ginny called the county prosecutor's office, after which she turned to Joe, "We're set for Porter in his office at three."

"Fantastic. I can't wait. Let's put those nine guilty clients from Wallerman's prosecutor days into a logical driving sequence."

"Yeah. Then we can grab lunch and head over to Porter's."

"Deal."

Joe and Ginny did just that. They had a late lunch and were in the county prosecutor's office at 2:50. Porter came out and greeted them a few minutes later.

Once they were all seated in Porter's office, he said, "I'm glad you scheduled this, Ginny. I was planning to call you guys this morning to get an update, but you beat me to it. So where are we?"

"Not as far as we'd like, but making progress," said Joe. He and Ginny then gave Porter the same update they'd given to the chief only a few hours earlier.

"Jeez, that's disappointing. What are your guts telling you?"

"Not too much yet," said Joe. "But despite striking out with the search this morning, we're still very interested in Harkness."

"That's good."

"We're expecting to get his location data dump in the

next couple of days. Hopefully, that'll put him at the crime scene at the right time."

"Good. Let me know what you learn."

"We also still have a large number of identified and unidentified possible suspects and several other possible motives. It'll take shoe leather and time to work through these."

"Shoe leather isn't my problem. Time is. The fact that the victim was a town councilman lifts this case to a level that gets a lot of visibility."

"We know. We're doing all we can, as fast as we can," said Ginny.

"I know you are. Hopefully you'll learn something useful at the AfA demo Friday evening."

"What AfA demo?" asked Joe.

"Don't you guys read a newspaper or watch the news? Or at least listen to the news while you're in your car?"

"Sometimes," said Ginny. "But I guess we've been too busy lately."

"Well the local chapter of AfA was granted a permit to stage a peaceful demonstration outside city hall Friday evening from six to nine."

"What, or who, is the AfA?" asked Ginny.

"America for Americans. It's a relatively new group that's been springing up. Mostly in Ohio, Pennsylvania, West Virginia and Kentucky."

"I gather from their name that they're anti-immigrant."

"Officially, they're anti-illegal, or as we say, undocumented, immigrants. In reality, they seem to be against all immigrants. And, for good measure, you can also toss in blacks, Hispanics, Muslims, Jews and Catholics."

"Nice to know they're not showing favoritism about who they hate," said Joe.

"They sound like the KKK of old, without the white sheets," said Ginny.

"Well said," Porter replied.

"What are they protesting about here?" asked Joe.

"The town council, with Wallerman leading the charge, looking into declaring Jasper Creek a sanctuary city, if you will, for illegal immigrants. This is not one of the AfA's most beloved proposals."

"No surprise there. Yes, we'll definitely be there on Friday. Never know what we'll hear or see. What can you tell us about their members and leadership, where they meet or have a headquarters and so on?"

"We've got almost half a file drawer full of info about them, the brochures they give out, and so on. I can find you a table with a couple of chairs and you're free to rummage through those files."

"Great. We'd like to do that now," said Ginny.

"OK, then. I'll have someone set you up and get you the files. And thanks for the update, despite the lack of much good news so far. Hope your suspect proves to be the perp. Or maybe this AfA will turn into a good lead."

"We'll see. Hope so. Thanks."

Five minutes later, Joe and Ginny were sitting at a table along the back wall of the bullpen where most of the paralegals worked. The files were piled on the table in front of them.

Joe and Ginny spent the next 90 minutes reading or at least quickly scanning everything in the files. They took notes and made copies of certain documents.

"OK," said Ginny. "Let's head back and see if we can make any sense out of all this." They returned the files and headed back to the station.

"Let's go over what we have about our new friends at the AfA," said Ginny. "Why don't you check with Patrol as well as our databases? I want to spend a few minutes checking the Internet."

"Will do. See you in a few."

While Ginny was searching the Internet and printing various items of possible interest, Joe was downstairs talking with the desk sergeant.

"Yeah, Joe. They're one of our newer pains in the butt. Nothing serious. Yet. Mostly bar fights and that kind of thing. But they seem to be gaining new members, and we're concerned about things getting out of control Friday night. We've arranged for additional resources from some of the neighboring towns and the state's Special Response Team."

"Good idea. Better safe than sorry. What do you have on their leaders, members, location, and so on?"

"Not much, but we loaded whatever we have into the all-knowing computer."

"Sounds like you're not a big computer fan, Sarge."

"Hell, I'm older than you, Joe. Whaddaya expect?"

"I'm with you on that. Hey, thanks for your help."

"No problem. Say hello to the pretty one of your partnership."

"Will do. Take care."

"Same to you."

Back upstairs, Ginny asked, "What did you learn?"

"Not much. But I think the sarge is in love with you."

"No. We just go way back. He was there when I started in Patrol. Anyway, I'm currently taken."

"Yeah, well, I didn't tell him that. He did say that AfA is a growing concern. Nothing serious yet, but . . . Whatever they have is in the computer database. Maybe you can check it. You know I'm no good at that stuff."

"Already did."

"And?"

"Their headquarters is in a rural area outside of Pittsburgh. Then there's the Ohio Brigade, if you will, headquartered outside Canton. The Jasper Creek chapter is really a very recent split off from the Columbus chapter. Probably 15 or 20 members here in Jasper Creek. But there's concern that members from elsewhere will join the demonstration on Friday. Not to mention who and how many will show up to protest against the AfA."

"Wow! Little, old Jasper Creek is making it to the big leagues. Too bad it's for such a crappy reason."

"Oh, by the way, got a call from a Bob Simmons at BCI while you were downstairs. They finished their ballistics work on the bullets. Confirmed that they're 10mm and both came from the same gun. If and when we get another bullet or a gun, they can compare bullet striations to determine if it's the same gun used to kill Wallerman."

"Great. All we need is to find that gun. Could use some big-time luck for that."

"Very true. But it is what it is. At least they did their work and called us. Hey, Joe, speaking of calls, if you agree, I'm going to give Councilwoman Gould a call. Just to make sure she's aware of Friday night and for her to be alert to her surroundings. She's been the only other outspoken sanctuary city proponent besides Wallerman. I want her to not be shy about calling 9-1-1 if she sees or suspects or even feels something unusual."

"Good idea, Ginny. And I'm going to make sure Patrol is making those few extra passes of her house every day and sitting out front whenever they can."

"Definitely worth double-checking."

Chapter 21

Joe and Ginny spent part of the next morning organizing all the material they had gathered about the AfA from the county prosecutor, from the desk sergeant and the department's computer files, and from the Internet.

Ginny then called Wallerman's paralegal to say that she and Joe would be stopping by later that morning.

Joe and Ginny arrived at Wallerman's office a few minutes after 10.

"Hello, Detectives. I owe you an apology."

"Yes?" said Ginny.

"I was supposed to go through our files and call you a few days ago. But going through all the files, along with other work to close down and transfer everything, is taking much longer than I thought."

"How far along are you?" asked Joe.

"Sadly, not much more than halfway."

"Did you start with the most recent or the oldest cases?" asked Joe.

"Unfortunately, neither. I did go through all the currently open cases. But the closed cases are filed alphabetically, not by date. So I've got a random mixture of recent and old."

"And of those you've gone through, how many have you identified as being worthy of our follow-up?"

"There are about 30 that I call very worthwhile, and another 40 or so that I labeled maybe."

"Wow," said Ginny. "That's quite a lot."

"Yes, but I haven't yet gone back through the older ones to see who was in prison or something until recently. That info's not in our files. It'll take a longer time to research it all, but I expect it'll bring the numbers way down."

"When do you expect to get through it all?" asked Joe.

"Hard to say. Mr. Collins keeps giving me special projects."

"Tell you what," said Ginny. "Why don't you give us the 30 worthwhile and 40 maybe names now? We'll work on checking if they were unavailable until recently. You keep working to get through the rest of the files."

"OK. That clearly will let me finish sooner."

"While we're here, we'd also like to talk some more about the various women Mr. Wallerman was dating."

"Like I told you last time, I really don't know much about them at all."

"Do you know any of their names?" asked Joe.

"No. Mr. Wallerman kept that pretty private."

"Didn't any of them ever call and give their name?"

"Well, yes. A few. But I don't remem. . . . Wait a second. If they called when Mr. Walllerman wasn't here or was in a meeting or on the phone, I would have taken a message."

"Yes? And?" asked Ginny.

"Our phone message pads have an original and a carbonless copy page for each message. That way, I could give the original message to Mr. Wallerman and still have a copy to help me double-check our client billings. Mr.

Wallerman charges his time in 10-minute increments, and that includes time on phone calls."

"Do you have those message copies for say the past six months?" asked Ginny.

"Sure. They're part of our official records. We retain them forever."

"Great. Can you get them now for the past six months? I'd like the three of us to go through them to see if we can identify some of the women."

"OK. Give me a few minutes to dig them out."

Joe, Ginny and Radner spent the next two and a half hours going through approximately 50 pads with the copies of all the messages. At one point, they briefly stopped and Radner ordered sandwiches to be delivered and made a fresh pot of coffee.

"Did Mr. Wallerman ever do anything but speak on the phone? I've never seen so many messages," said Ginny.

"Well, that is a large part of practicing law. And don't forget, there're no messages for all the times that Mr. Wallerman was able to take the call when it came in. Or for all the calls he placed."

Radner was able to recognize and eliminate almost all of the calls on the message pads, which were from other lawyers, the courthouse, clients and potential clients. When they were finished, they were left with nine messages, all from women whose names Radner didn't recognize. Some had a first and last name, others just a first name. And seven of the nine had a return phone number. Not wanting to mess up her retention system, Radner had put a sticky note on each of the nine. When they were finished, she made photocopies of the nine for Joe and Ginny.

"Ms. Radner, thank you very much. We appreciate your time. This has been very helpful."

"You're welcome. Glad I was able to help."

"One other thing," said Joe.

"Yes?"

"We'd like to borrow Mr. Wallerman's agenda or datebook for the past six months. We'd like to look for these or other women's names, most likely during evenings and weekends."

"OK. But you need to return it to me."

"We definitely will," said Ginny.

A few minutes later, Joe and Ginny were out the door, Wallerman's agenda and copies of the nine phone messages in their hands.

Back at their desks, Joe and Ginny spent almost an hour checking each of the names Wallerman's paralegal had given them against all the names they had gotten from Jane Daniels in the prosecutor's office. They found five hits, indicating that Wallerman had involvement with these people both when he worked in the prosecutor's office and when he had his own law firm. These names were moved to the top of their list for follow-up.

Joe and Ginny spent the remainder of that day and most of Friday meeting with those whose names were on both lists as well as a few of the serious-crime convicts whom Wallerman had convicted while an assistant prosecutor and who had recently been released from prison. None of those who Joe and Ginny spoke with seemed to be likely suspects.

Chapter 22

Joe and Ginny returned to the station around four o'clock and began prepping for the AfA demonstration. They reviewed the notes and photocopies from the prosecutor's files and the information Ginny had gotten from the PD's database.

"Ginny, I've got no real evidence, but my gut's telling me that this AfA group, or even a nonmember riled up about illegal immigrants, may prove to be the key."

"Could be, but if not, I'm betting on either Harkness or one of Wallerman's girlfriends. These seem more likely than someone, other than Harkness, with a grudge from a court case years ago."

"I'm with you on that. We can't totally discard the old-case possibility, but the motive coming from a more current situation seems more likely. And that means this illegal-immigration, sanctuary city thing, or one of his so-called flings as you said one of his neighbors called them. Plus, of course, our good friend Harkness."

"Agreed. Joe, let's head over to city hall now so we can get a nice viewing area. Hope we see something useful. I'd hate to stand there for four hours for nada."

"You and me both. At least we have access into city hall for potty breaks."

"Thank heaven for little things."

By five o'clock, Joe and Ginny were across the street

from City Hall, watching the AfA members, as well as their supporters and detractors, starting to arrive.

"So far, it looks like there're more than enough cops and troopers here," said Ginny.

"Yup, so far. Let's hope it stays that way."

Joe and Ginny surveyed the whole area, and decided to stand at the top of the steps into city hall, selecting the far right-hand edge. This would give them a good overview of the demonstrators, who would be facing city hall, while being far enough off to one side so as not to be the focus of the demonstrators' attention.

"Ginny, is this about over yet?"

"Almost, Joe. It's already 5:20, and this is scheduled for six to nine."

"You call that 'almost?'"

"I'll call it anything you like if you promise not to cry."

"Well, I'll try real hard not to."

"That's such a good boy."

"Hey, Ginny. See that guy in the black coat. He looks like one of the leaders, if not *the* leader."

"I'm taking a lot of pictures with my cell. I'll be sure to get a clear one of him."

"Luckily, most of the spectators are taking photos. You don't look out of place doing the same thing."

"Joe, look at the sign that lady in green is carrying. 'Town Council, how about when an illegal kills YOUR family?' Jeez. Talk about being direct."

"You don't have to agree with them, but their point about illegal immigrants does make some sense. Too bad so many of these groups then extend their thinking to include legal immigrants and a slew of other minority groups."

"Yeah. I think when you start to hate, it's like melted butter."

"Huh? Melted butter?"

"Exactly. It starts to spread out and it's damn near impossible to contain."

"Got it. Good analogy, Ginny. Even though I needed an explanation."

"Do you need me to spread it out for you?"

"Ha. Ha. Very funny."

Joe and Ginny watched the crowd grow.

"Given the number of participants, many of the protestors have to be AfA members from other areas or just nonmembers who are against Jasper Creek becoming a sanctuary city."

"True. And there are at least as many across the street who are in favor of the sanctuary thing. I guess you could describe them as protesting the protestors."

"Yes. I'm watching them as well, but one of them is unlikely to be the killer, if the killer's motivation was being against JC becoming a sanctuary city."

"Agreed."

The actual demonstration began a few minutes past six. Several individuals, mostly men but also a few women, took turns standing up with a megaphone and making speeches, running anywhere from five to 15 minutes. Several of them finished by encouraging the crowd to join in a series of chants. "America for Americans," or "Illegal Immigration is Illegal," or "Go Back Home and

Get in Line." Since most of the speakers walked up some of the steps before turning around to face the crowd, Ginny was able to get clear photos of their faces before they started to speak.

Joe and Ginny took special note of a few of the speakers who seemed most extreme in supporting a tough line against illegal immigrants. A few focused on localities having a duty to enforce federal laws, but most talked about rapes and murders that these "illegals" would commit, thereby destroying the safety and sense of community of the entire town.

The greater the enthusiasm of the demonstrators, the greater the enthusiasm of the pro-sanctuary crowd across the street. The police managed to keep the two groups separated, so that both the protest and the anti-protest remained peaceful, albeit loud. Joe took two breaks to go into city hall to use the restroom. And Joe filled as photographer the few times Ginny made similar city hall visits. As the police officers at the door knew both Joe and Ginny, they didn't even have to show their badges to gain entry.

The crowd began to disperse by 8:30.

"Joe, looks like it's dying down. Not sure there's much more left to see."

"I agree. Let's give it a few more minutes, then head back to our cars. What's on the schedule for this weekend?"

"Good question. Haven't really had a chance all week to think about it. What would you like to do?"

"No idea. Hold on. Let me check the forecast."

"Good idea, Joe."

"Looks like no rain. Sunny or partly sunny. Highs in the mid-50s. OK. It's settled then."

"Settled? What? Settled on what?"

"It's obvious, Ginny."

"Well, not to me. Clue me in."

"Happy to. We get up early tomorrow and head to Cincinnati for the weekend."

"Cincinnati? How'd you come up with that?"

"Damned if I know. It just came to me. I've been there several times, but always on PD business. It seems like a nice city with lots of parks and museums and stuff."

"OK. Let's do it then," said Ginny. "I've also been there, but never to play tourist."

"Why don't you stay at my place so we can get an early start in the morning?"

"OK. But I'm starving right now."

"We'll go in two cars. I'll lead you to one of the better Jasper Creek pizza joints."

"Deal."

And that's what they did. Pizza and a couple of beers each, followed by an hour of TV back at Joe's house and into bed.

Chapter 23

The next morning, Joe and Ginny were on the road by 7:30. The first stop was at a McDonald's drive-through window for breakfast in the car. Along the way, Ginny used her smart phone to check a few hotels in Cincinnati. After conferring with Joe, she made a reservation at a Hampton Inn in downtown Cincinnati. The whole drive, including the McDonald's stop, took just under two hours.

Arriving at the hotel before their room was ready, they left their overnight bags at the front desk, obtained a city map and suggestions of what not to miss, and headed out to play tourist.

They enjoyed the day. Visiting the zoo, two museums and a few parks and trails, their minds were completely free of police business until late in the day. Lounging in their room later in the afternoon, they went over the photos and notes they had taken at the demonstration the evening before.

"Ginny, you sure took a lot of photos."

"Yeah. More than I thought I did. It's so simple with your cellphone, you tend to just shoot away."

"I can see that. Now what do we do with all the photos you took?"

"Well, I tried to get good head shots of all the speakers, who presumably were the leaders of the group. I also tried to get anyone who seemed exceptionally emotional, as well as those who seemed to be standing back, alone, sort of away from the crowd."

"Not to mention the photos you took of those protesting the protest."

"Yeah, but I think we can ignore them for the time being."

"Can't argue with your impeccable logic. But back to my earlier question. What do we do with the photos you took of the demonstrators?"

"OHLEG."

"Huh? What the heck is that? A disease? Does your leg hurt? Or is it a new curse word?"

"Very funny, Joe. No, it stands for Ohio Law Enforcement Gateway."

"OK. And I stand by my question. What the heck is it? Gateway to what?"

"It's the new system offered by BCI that gives all police departments in the state access to BCI's facial recognition software and database."

"Oh, yeah. I've seen some stuff about that. But I've never used it. You haven't either, have you?"

"Nope. This'll be a first for me. But I've read about it. It seems pretty simple. We upload our photos into their system, and the computer compares details of the person's face to the more than 21 million photos in their database."

"Twenty-one million? That's like twice the population of Ohio."

"Yeah. They have multiple photos of many people. From DMV license applications, arrests and so on."

"I'm looking forward to seeing this. It sounds almost like science fiction."

"I guess it was science fiction until a few years ago. Anyhow, when we're back at the station on Monday, I'll give it a shot."

"Also, we need to start trying to decipher the phone messages and Wallerman's datebook to identify some of his girlfriends."

"I agree, Joe. But is your main reason to help solve the case or to get the names of some local, young, attractive and apparently available females?" asked Ginny with a grin.

"How could you even think such a thing?" asked Joe as he put on his very best shocked-face look. "You should know that my extracurricular activities are limited to someone named Virginia Harris."

"That's what I've heard. Just checking to be sure that the rumors are true."

"Just what any good detective would do."

"OK, Joe. But now it's time to get back to our weekend."

"Time to shower and dress and head out to dinner. I saw an ad for a special steakhouse and made a reservation for seven o'clock."

"Fine with me. What makes it so special?"

"It's exactly right for us."

"OK, quit teasing, Joe. What's the deal?"

"OK. OK. The name of the restaurant is 'The Precinct.' It's in an old police station."

"Really? That's wild. I gotta see this."

"Me too. And, the food also gets top-notch reviews."

"Sounds like a winner. I'm heading for a bath now. You can shower as soon as I'm done."

"OK. But you'll need to shorten your normal four-hour soak, or we'll miss dinner."

"It won't be easy, but I'll try to cut it back to 3½ hours."

Ginny, in fact, was out of the bathroom after 15 minutes. Joe and Ginny arrived 10 minutes early at the restaurant. They enjoyed their meal. The food was delicious, the building and dining room were unique. Joe and Ginny totally relaxed and forgot all about work, their concerns about their relationship relative to the chief, and everything else except each other.

Back at the hotel, Joe and Ginny had a couple of nightcaps in the small bar area off to one corner of the lobby. Then it was up to their room, after which they tumbled into bed.

They slept until eight o'clock the next morning, an infrequent indulgence for them. They quickly dressed, went downstairs and enjoyed a buffet breakfast. Ginny ate very little, reminding Joe of the large dinner the night before. Joe stuffed himself, explaining that what they ate the day before had nothing to do with this day; each day started off with a clean slate, or as Joe said, "a clean plate."

After breakfast, they checked out of the hotel and loaded their bags into the car, but they left the car in the parking garage. They rented bikes and spent a few hours biking around downtown and along the riverfront. The city was unusually peaceful, with very little traffic, given that it was Sunday morning. Around 11:30, they stopped at a sandwich shop for a pleasant lunch. It was then time to return the bikes, grab the car and head back to Jasper Creek.

They arrived back in Jasper Creek in time to grill a simple dinner at Joe's, and ended the weekend with an early bedtime, nestled together.

Chapter 24

The next morning, Ginny left first and Joe followed a few minutes later.

When Joe reached his desk, Ginny was already sitting at hers with two cups of hot coffee.

"Here, Joe. It's hot and still reasonably fresh," said Ginny as she handed one of the cups to Joe.

"Thanks, Partner."

"I'm reviewing that article about facial recognition. Looks pretty easy. BCI's online system gives you step-by-step instructions."

"Good. I'm watching."

"OK. It only analyzes one face at a time. I'll start with the leaders and oddballs I photographed. Afterwards, we can have it also do searches for some of the faces in the crowd."

"Go for it. Sure am glad you're nimble with all this computer mumbo jumbo."

"That's natural given how much younger I am than you."

"Gimme a break. Hey, before you start, let me run and get the chief. I bet he's never used nor seen this before."

"Good idea. I'm sure he hasn't. I don't think he's even come to grips yet with the fact that you can take pictures with your cellphone."

"See. I'm not the most technically backward person in the state."

"Just think of yourself as a nerd in training."

"Very funny. Let me go grab the chief."

Joe and the chief were standing behind Ginny less than five minutes later.

"OK, here goes," said Ginny as she pulled up the state's Bureau of Criminal Investigation's website, registered with a name and password, and uploaded the first photo from her cellphone.

Within a few minutes, the computer stopped comparing the photo to those in its database. It showed three different photos of a man, whom it identified as Steven Howard.

"What? That was quick," said the chief. "But those three photos don't look like the same person."

"They are. I'm sure," said Ginny. "We're thrown off by the beard in the second photo and the fact that he's a lot heavier in the third shot."

"So how'd the computer see past all that?" asked the chief.

"The system doesn't address, or even know, what the person looks like. It compares a bunch of static data that doesn't change. Like the exact distance between his eyes, the exact width of his nose, the depth of the eye sockets and so on."

"Pretty amazing," said Joe.

Ginny then clicked on a few more boxes to get information about Steven Howard.

"Looks like one of Jasper Creek's finest. Three years for armed robbery, six months for assault and battery, and a bunch of other minor offenses."

"Yup. Definitely earns a spot on our to-be-visited list."

"This sure looks like a neat tool," said the chief. "Thanks for showing it to me. Glad we got someone in the department who knows how to use it."

"It's real simple, Chief. I'd be happy to explain it to everyone at one of our training sessions."

"Good idea, Ginny. Now check your other photos and then, hopefully, nail the perp."

"That's our plan," said Joe.

The chief returned to his office, while Ginny printed out all the information and the three photos, along with the last-known address, for Howard.

"Pretty neat, Ginny. Should we submit your next photo?"

"Yup. Just about to."

Ginny, with Joe watching most of the time, spent the rest of the day entering photos into the facial recognition system. They asked one of the other officers who was going out for lunch to bring back lunch for them. Ginny kept working on the photos while she and Joe gulped down their Quarter Pounders and fries.

Following lunch, Joe said, "Ginny, I'm going to break off for a few minutes."

"Need a nap after that gourmet lunch?"

"Ha, ha. No. Actually, I want to do some checking into Wallerman's three heirs. In addition to checking for rap sheets and DMV convictions, I want to get a better handle on when each of them learned that they'd be inheriting a small fortune."

"Good idea, Joe."

Joe called Wallerman's executor. David Collins was on a conference call that was expected to go for another hour or so. Joe left a message asking Collins to call him back.

While waiting, Joe checked into the background of Wallerman's two ex-wives. Although he didn't view her as a serious suspect, he also did the same for Wallerman's paralegal. In all three cases, he found nothing more damning than a few several-years-ago speeding tickets.

When Collins did call him back, Joe explained that he wanted to better understand when each of the heirs learned of their good fortune, and, specifically, had any of them known before Wallerman's death that they were to be his heirs.

"Detective, I, of course, can't be 100 percent certain that Carl hadn't told any of them. I can be, and am, sure that neither I nor any of my staff ever said anything to anyone. We've been together for years, and confidentiality has never been a problem here. And, although I again can't be 100 percent sure, I'm pretty certain that none of the heirs knew or even suspected this before Carl's death. Based on my many years of having these in-person meetings to inform heirs, I'm convinced that all three ladies were truly surprised, or even shocked. At being an heir and, of course, at the estimated size of their inheritance."

"Mr. Collins, thank you. Your comments have been most helpful."

"You're very welcome. Any time."

After hanging up, Joe brought Ginny up to date. Both agreed that all three heirs were unlikely suspects.

A few hours later, Ginny said, "OK, Joe, that's it."

"Well done. You must be beat after doing that all day."

"Yeah, my eyes are blurry and burning. But we got some good stuff. We entered 21 photos of people I focused on, plus about 50 from various crowd shots."

"Good thing we can use the system for free."

"You bet. Otherwise, we, or the department, would be a lot poorer than we were this morning."

"Right. So how many were hits?"

"Let's see. Of the 21 I selected, the system identified 14. Of those, nine were clean and five had one or more felony convictions."

"We won't throw 'em away, but we'll move the clean boy scouts to the bottom of our follow-up list."

"Full agreement. And of the 50 or so from crowd shots, 22 were identified. Of these, 10 had felony convictions."

"OK. We've got some work ahead of us. But that's for tomorrow."

"Agreed. I'll see you in the A.M., Joe. I need a night to unwind and catch up on my sleep."

"Understood. Have a good night, Ginny."

"Thanks. Ditto to you."

Chapter 25

The next morning, Joe and Ginny spent the first 90 minutes or so organizing by address all the people from the AfA demonstration they wanted to follow up on. This would allow them to make the visits in a logical and efficient sequence. Six of the 15 identified for follow-up listed last-known addresses in other Ohio towns and cities. These were put at the bottom of the pile.

"OK, Ginny. Let's get started. Number one is a Mark Netter. He's in the northeast corner."

"OK. A pit stop and coffee refill, and I'm good to go."

"My thoughts exactly," said Joe.

Twenty minutes later, Joe parked in front of a small bungalow-like house. Light gray, but in dire need of a paint job, the house was as unattractive as the small, weed-overgrown lawn. Joe and Ginny walked up the severely cracked and crumbling concrete walk. Joe rang the doorbell. When no one responded, Joe knocked loudly on the door.

"Yeah. Yeah. Hold your horses. I'm coming."

A minute later, Mark Netter was standing in front of the door. About 40 years old and in desperate need of a shave, Netter was wearing a pair of old, stained jeans and a yellowed T-shirt. His hair looked like it hadn't been touched by a comb for at least a few days."

"Mark Netter?" asked Joe.

"Who wants to know?"

"We do. I'm Detective McFarland and this is Detective Harris. Jasper Creek PD."

"Whaddaya think I did now?"

"Perhaps nothing," said Ginny. "We just want to talk with you. May we come in for a few minutes?"

"Uh. Yeah, I guess so. But the place ain't as neat as it usually is."

"That's not a problem," said Ginny.

Netter let them in and led them to the back of the house where they all sat down around the kitchen table.

"So whaddaya wanna talk about? Baseball?"

"'Fraid not," said Joe. "Were you at the demonstration outside city hall Friday night?"

"Yeah. What about it? Nothin' illegal about that."

"That's true," said Ginny. "Can you tell us why you were there?"

"Sure. To protest that damn sanctuary city crap."

"Can you be more specific?" asked Joe.

"Yeah. The stupid town council is going to make Jasper Creek a sanctuary city."

"And I take it you're against that?" asked Ginny.

"Damn right. Instead of kicking their asses out of the country, we're gonna invite 'em here and cuddle 'em and give 'em stuff. That's bull."

"Why?" asked Joe.

"Hell, I can't even find a job right now. And we're gonna let those criminals come here. They're willing to work for next to nothing, so no one's ever gonna hire me. And while I'm collecting my measly unemployment checks, they're getting all kinds of bennies from the city and all the churches and other do-gooders. How about they take care of us Americans before they help all the un-Americans coming here?"

"You seem to feel pretty strong about that," said Ginny.

"You would too if they took your job and then got all the support on top of that."

"Where were you two Mondays ago? Say from eight to midnight."

"How should I remember? That was two weeks ago."

"Well, try real hard."

"Can't specifically remember. But I'd guess right here. I'm not exactly doing a lot of socializing and going out these days."

"Mr. Netter, are you a member of America for Americans?" asked Joe.

"No. I agree with a lot of their points, but I ain't the joiner type. I know they organized that thing in front of city hall. I went, but I ain't no member."

"Mr. Netter, what are your thoughts about Mr. Wallerman?" asked Ginny. "He was a member of the town council."

"Oh, yeah. He was the guy that was murdered in his house. What's that got to do with me?"

"Any idea why he might have been killed?" asked Joe.

"No."

"Or who might have done it?"

"No idea. Why you asking me about that?"

"Well, we think he might have been killed because he was one of those proposing that we become a sanctuary city."

"Right. And cuz I'm an ex-con, I must have done it."

"No, Mr. Netter," said Ginny. "We're checking with people like you who were at that demonstration to see if they might have heard anything about his murder from other people there."

"Well, I didn't hear nothing."

"OK, Mr. Netter. That'll be it for now. Here are our cards. Please call if you think of anything else. Also call us before you leave the state."

"Yeah, sure. I'll definitely call you before I go on my next worldwide cruise."

Joe and Ginny said their goodbyes and were soon back in their car.

"That's one pissed-off guy," said Ginny.

"Agreed. I can't decide if I dislike him or feel sorry for him. Maybe both. Anyhow, I didn't get any suspicious vibes? You?"

"Me neither. Let's head to our next one. That'll be Steven Howard, the first guy identified while we were showing the system to the chief. Howard doesn't live far from here."

Within a few minutes, they were knocking on the door of unit 225 of a small, but well-kept group of garden apartments.

"Yes?" said a voice from behind the door.

"We're with the Jasper Creek PD. We'd like to speak with Steven Howard."

"That's me. One second."

Howard opened the door. Introductions were made, and Joe and Ginny followed Howard into his living room. Everyone took a seat.

"What's this about?"

"Mr. Howard, were you at the demonstration Friday night?"

"Yeah. Why? I'm allowed. I even checked with my parole officer before I went."

"Mr. Howard, how come you went?" asked Ginny.

"To support them."

"Who?"

"The people who were against the protesters. I think that sanctuary stuff is a good idea."

"You do?" asked Joe.

"Yeah. Unless you're an Indian, I mean an American Indian, if there wasn't immigration you wouldn't be here. I'm not one of those people who gets in and then wants to lock the door so others can't follow. I was lucky. So give other people the same chance."

"Were you part of an organized group?"

"Nah. It was just people who felt like me. And the cops had us stay across the street. They didn't want any fights between us and those people against the sanctuary stuff."

"During most of the demonstration, you were standing all the way in the back. All by yourself."

"Yeah. So?"

"Just wondering why you weren't more involved with the other sanctuary-city supporters," said Joe.

"Well, I didn't know anyone who was there. And I'm not keen on making new friends. So I just stood where I did."

"Understood. Mr. Howard, do you know about Mr. Wallerman, the town council member who was killed?"

"Sure. It was all over the news for days. Why?"

"We think he might have been killed by someone against his sanctuary city proposal," said Ginny.

"Oh. Well that lets me off the hook. Cause I'm in favor of it."

"Did you see anything, or hear anything, suspicious while you were at the demonstration?"

"No. Just the demonstrators and us. And yelling back and forth."

"Mr. Howard," said Ginny. "Just for the record, where were you when Mr. Wallerman was killed? That would have been Monday evening, two weeks ago."

"I'm sure I was here. During the week, I'm home every night. Dinner, some TV and then in bed around 10."

"Is there anyone who can corroborate that?" asked Joe.

"No. I'm sure I was here just by myself."

"OK, Mr. Howard," said Ginny. "Thank you for your time. Here are our cards if you think of anything else."

Back in the car, Joe said, "Well, that surprised me. With his rap sheet and prison time, I was sure we'd have a live one here."

"Me too. But I think he's in the clear. Even though he has no alibi, he was on the other team."

They struck out at the next two locations. One was a boarded-up, dilapidated house. Their person of interest either had lived there many years earlier or had given a false address that the authorities never checked out. The second house looked lived in, but no one was home. Two neighbors confirmed that a man lived there alone and was away every weekday for work, but that they didn't know where.

After a quick stop for lunch at McDonald's, they headed toward the southeast part of town.

Their one stop was very short. Their suspect had an excellent alibi for the night of the murder. He had been downtown bar hopping, got very drunk and was arrested while urinating on the steps in front of city hall. Ginny called the desk sergeant and he checked and confirmed his story. Spending the whole night in jail definitely precluded him from being the killer.

Their next stop was to check on someone living on the southwest side of town. A neighbor told Joe and Ginny that he had left town a few days ago to visit his sister in Tennessee. The neighbor thought he'd be back home in another week or so.

Their next stop was due west of downtown, just about two blocks before the town line, beyond which was unincorporated county territory. Although this was inside the city limits, the area looked more like the unincorporated rural parts of the county. Small, mostly rundown houses sitting on multi-acre lots. Suburbia clearly hadn't reached this far out yet.

Finding the house by the number on the rusty, dented mailbox at the end of the driveway, Joe turned in and followed the dirt drive for about 500 feet. At the end of the driveway was what appeared to be a one- or two-room log cabin.

"Wow. This feels like we're in the back hills of Wyoming, not a part of Jasper Creek," said Ginny.

"I know exactly what you mean. The good news is that the smoke coming from the chimney means that our boy is probably at home."

"Yup. Let's go see. This should be interesting. This guy was identified as the head of the up-and-coming Jasper Creek chapter of the AfA."

The front door opened when Joe and Ginny were still about 25 feet away.

"Whatever you're sellin', I'm not interested."

"We're not selling anything," answered Joe.

"Mr. Unger? Frederick Unger?" asked Ginny.

"Yeah. So what?"

"We're with the police department. We'd like to ask you a few questions."

"'Bout what?"

"May we come in, Mr. Unger?" asked Ginny.

"I'd rather we do this out here."

"Fair enough. I'm Detective Harris and this is Detective McFarland."

"And?"

"We'd like to talk to you about America for Americans."

"Yeah, what about it? Nothing illegal about it. You two wanting to become members?"

"No. But thank you," said Joe. "Are you the head of the local Jasper Creek chapter?"

"Sort of."

"What does that mean?"

"I'm temporarily head of it. I helped start the local chapter and I'm running it for now. Once we get more members, we'll have an election to officially select our officers."

"How many members do you currently have?" asked Ginny.

"About 15. But we got a whole bunch of people who're

interested. So I expect a lot of new members signing up real soon."

"I see," said Joe. "What can you tell us about the demonstration Friday night?"

"Whaddaya want to know?"

"Did you organize it?"

"Well, I helped. But the whole chapter really organized it. And a few members from other chapters helped us. Why? We got the required permit and stuff for the demonstration."

"Yes, we're aware of that. What exactly was the demonstration about?" asked Ginny.

"The town council's thinking of making Jasper Creek a sanctuary city. Can you imagine that?"

"And I take it you and your group are against that."

"Hell yes. We ought to be sending those creatures back to where they came from."

"Those are pretty strong words, Mr. Unger," said Joe.

"Yeah, well, we feel pretty strongly about it. I mean legal immigrants are bad enough, but we're talking about illegal immigrants. Illegal. I'm sure that's something that detectives understand. They're criminals. We should either send 'em back home or lock 'em up. We sure as hell shouldn't coddle and encourage 'em."

"Mr. Unger, what do you know about Carl Wallerman?" asked Joe.

"He was one of the instigators of this on the town council. Fortunately, he was murdered before he could do too much damage."

"Do you really mean *fortunately*?"

"You bet I do. But before you bother asking, that doesn't mean I killed him."

"Any idea who might have?"

"Nope."

"One of your members perhaps?"

"We feel strongly about this issue. But we don't kill people. We only use peaceful methods."

"Mind telling us where you were when Mr. Wallerman was killed?"

"When exactly was that?"

"It was two Mondays ago. In the evening," said Ginny.

"Not sure, but, if I had to guess, I'd say I was right here."

"Anyone here with you? Someone who can vouch for that?" asked Ginny.

"Maybe some of our members. Maybe not. Hard to tell one day from the next. I don't keep a big fancy written schedule for my activities."

"As you might imagine, that's not the best alibi we've ever heard," said Joe.

"Well, it is what it is."

"So, tell me," said Joe, "if Mr. Wallerman was the main proponent of this on the town council, why'd you demonstrate after he was killed?"

"We wanna make sure the council drops this stupid idea."

"And you had evidence that they weren't going to stop?"

"No real evidence. But once something gets started, no telling what politicians might do. Plus that Wallerman guy had a sidekick on the council, a damn woman, and she might continue pushing this issue."

"Are you sure that the killer couldn't be one of your members?" asked Ginny.

"Sure? Hell no. I'm not even totally sure the sun'll come up tomorrow. I don't know most of these members real well. I'm just saying America for Americans doesn't support or encourage violence."

"Did you notice anyone at the demonstration, AfA member or not, who seemed in any way suspicious?"

"Nope. Except for the damn politicians. I'm always real suspicious of them."

"OK, Mr. Unger. That's it for now. We may be back if we have more questions."

"Why aren't I surprised? If you change your mind and would like to join, let me know. We'd be happy to have you."

"Thanks, but don't hold your breath."

"Here are our cards," said Ginny. "Call us if you think of anything else. Also, be sure to call us before you leave the state."

"Are you telling me I'm a suspect in that guy's murder?"

"No," answered Ginny. "But for now, you're not a non-suspect either."

Joe and Ginny walked back to the car.

"I say we put this guy Unger up near the top of our list, maybe right next to Harkness. Just two more to catch today, Joe. One in the northwest of town, and one living in a flophouse in the rundown section downtown."

"OK. What's the address in the northwest?"

Ginny gave Joe the address, and he entered it into the GPS system in his cellphone. Fifteen minutes later, they were sitting in front of an empty field.

"Well, unless he's a groundhog, this is a phony address. There's no question about it. We just passed 224 and up ahead is 230. So 228 has to be on this lot."

"Yeah. I'm sure it will be. Whenever it's eventually built."

"OK, Ginny. We'll need to find this guy. Phony addresses are a red flag in my book."

"Mine also. Let's head downtown and try to see our last fellow of the day."

Ginny gave Joe the address. Joe was familiar enough with that rundown section of town that he didn't need his GPS to get there.

"Here we are. The Piedmont Hotel. Doesn't sound too bad until you see it. Not sure if the hotel or the area is in worse shape."

"Joe. I vote for a tie. They're both pretty bad. I know all bigger cities have a so-called bad part of town, but I always find it surprising that even a small town like Jasper Creek has one."

"Maybe that means Jasper Creek is moving up in the world. Let's head on in."

Joe and Ginny walked in, right up to the front desk. But no one was there. Ginny knocked on the desk, but no answer.

Joe then yelled, "Hello. Anyone here?"

"Hold on. Hold on. I'll be right there," came a voice from a back room.

A couple of minutes later, a tall, old man walked out from the back room, still pulling up and buttoning his pants. His hair was long and wild, his mouth close to toothless and his thin body badly slumped forward.

"Sorry about that. But when nature calls, you gotta

answer. Oh sorry, ma'am, I didn't see there was a lady here. By the way, we don't take no credit cards. And you gotta rent the room for at least two hours. And pay up front."

"We're not here for a room." Joe added, "We're Detectives McFarland and Harris," as he and Ginny both held up their badges.

"Oh, sorry, Detectives. What can I do for you?"

"What room is Alan Coletti in?" asked Ginny.

"He's up on the third floor. 308. Why? What's he done?"

"Nothing that we know of. We just want to talk with him. How long has he been staying here?"

"Don't know exactly. Couple of months or so."

"Is he in his room now?"

"Sure. He's almost always in his room. Only goes out maybe an hour or two each day."

"OK. Thanks. Don't call and tell him we're going up to see him," said Joe.

"Couldn't if I wanted to. No phones in the rooms. One payphone over there. That's it," he said as he nodded to the other end of the so-called lobby.

"OK."

Joe and Ginny walked up two flights in the dirty, litter-strewn stairway. They turned right and found room 308 most of the way down the hall on the right. They knocked on the door. And knocked again when no one answered.

"Yeah?"

"Mr. Coletti?"

"Yeah."

"Mr. Coletti, open the door. We're with the police department."

"Oh shit. That ain't never good. Gimme a minute to get my pants on."

Almost five minutes later, they heard someone shuffling across the room, and then the door opened.

"Why you here?"

"Mr. Coletti, may we come in?" asked Ginny.

"Yeah. I guess so." Coletti shuffled to one side so that Joe and Ginny could open the door further and walk into the room.

Before they even looked at the room, Joe and Ginny were overwhelmed by the smell. A combination of stuffiness, alcohol and body odor. Ginny glanced around and was amazed at where someone would live. A narrow bed, a three-drawer chest, a bridge table with two folding chairs, an ancient refrigerator, a sink and a hot plate totally filled the room. Judging from the pile of dirty clothing on the floor and the piles of dirty dishes in the sink and on the table, Ginny guessed that washing wasn't Coletti's strong suit.

Joe immediately realized that Coletti was drunk, which was probably his normal state. There was an open bottle of cheap brandy on the table. The lack of a glass indicated that Coletti did his drinking straight from the bottle. Coletti's shaking hands, reddish face and vein-covered nose only reinforced Joe's conclusion.

"Mr. Coletti, did you attend the demonstration at city hall last Friday night?" asked Joe.

"Huh?"

"Were you part of the demonstration on Friday?"

"There's a demonstration? About what?"

"Mr. Coletti," said Ginny, "we have a photo of you at that demonstration last Friday."

"Then I guess I was there."

"You don't remember?"

"Not no demonstration. Sometimes I walk around and see bunches of people. Maybe that was it."

"Yes, that probably was what it was. Thank you for your time," said Ginny.

"Any time. Thanks for stopping by."

Joe and Ginny made a quick exit and drove back to the station.

"Well, that was quite a day," said Joe as he and Ginny sat down at their desks.

"Sure was. But we did make some progress. Clearly that Unger fellow, head of the local AfA chapter, is at the top end of our list. That first person, the ex-con Howard, is on our list, but near the bottom. And that fellow, Netter, not to mention our friendly drunk, is also low on our list."

"Agreed. And we need to go back to the guy at work and the one visiting his sister."

"Yeah. And we need to chase down those two with nonexistent addresses."

"Well, that's what tomorrow's for. What say, how about my place tonight?"

"Works for me, Joe. I'll grab a pizza and some beer on the way over. See you in about 45 minutes."

"OK. I'll be waiting. I'm looking forward to the beer and pizza. And, oh yeah, to seeing you also."

"Great. Glad I made your list."

Joe and Ginny managed to avoid talking about the case over their pizza and stayed off that topic through two TV shows. By the end of the second show, they were too drowsy to talk about anything.

Chapter 26

J oe and Ginny were back at their desks by seven the next morning, enjoying freshly made coffee for a change.

"Joe, we've got an awful lot to cover today. Let's figure out a plan and schedule."

"OK. Lunch at noon."

"Seriously, Joe."

"I know. Just teasing. I think first thing we should update the chief. Then we want to track down those two from yesterday who gave false addresses."

"Yeah. Plus the one who was at work yesterday. I think we should also touch base with that councilwoman, Mrs. Gould, to remind her to stay vigilant and to see if anything's going on."

"Yup. And then we still have to follow up on some of those letter writers, as well as all the names from cases we got from Wallerman's paralegal. And we have to start digging in on identifying some of those girlfriends."

"Wow. We have enough for today and tomorrow, Joe. And the next day."

"Guess we'd better get started."

"OK. The chief's not in yet. Let's take a quick ride out to that guy who we missed yesterday because he was at work. We should be able to catch him before he leaves home."

"Good idea. That way we don't have to call him and give him time to dream up an alibi."

Although rush hour traffic into Jasper Creek was picking up, Joe and Ginny were going against the traffic and, in less than 15 minutes, they arrived at Harvey Bunting's house, a small, rundown, vinyl-sided cottage, probably 40 years old. They walked to the front door and rang the bell.

"Yes?"

"Mr. Bunting."

"Yes, that's me."

"We're with the Jasper Creek Police Department. We'd like to speak with you for a few minutes."

Bunting opened the door. "What's this about? I gotta leave for work soon."

"Mr. Bunting," said Ginny, "this won't take long. May we come in?"

"OK. But we gotta make it quick. Come with me to the kitchen so I can finish my breakfast. Want some toast? I don't have time to make more coffee."

"No, thanks. We're fine," said Joe.

"Mr. Bunting, were you at the America for Americans demonstration at city hall last Friday?"

"Yes, I was. Why?"

"Are you a member of AfA?" asked Joe.

"No. At least not yet. I got some pamphlets and stuff. I'm thinking of joining."

"Oh," said Ginny.

"Yeah. So I went to that demonstration to try to learn more about them."

"And?" prompted Ginny.

"I'm pretty sure I'm gonna join. All these immigrants, most who are illegal, are taking our jobs. And even if they don't take our jobs, they're willing to work for peanuts and that makes our pay go down."

"Mr. Bunting, has that happened to you?"

"No, thank God. Not yet."

"Mr. Bunting," said Joe, "are you aware of the killing of Councilman Wallerman?"

"Sure. Anyone who reads a paper or watches the news is. It's been in the news almost every day."

"Did you see or hear anything at the AfA demonstration that dealt with the killing?"

"No, not really. There was a lot of talk about that sanctuary city idea. And that Wallerman and some councilman lady was pushing it, but that's about it."

"Mr. Bunting," said Ginny, "just so we can clear the record, where were you when Mr. Wallerman was killed?"

"Uh. No idea. When exactly was he killed?"

"Monday evening, two weeks ago."

"Oh, that's easy then. I've been working a lot of overtime every Monday and Tuesday for the past six weeks. Almost a whole second shift. My regular shift's over at four. Then I've been working six overtime hours. Like I said, every Monday and Tuesday."

"Mr. Bunting," said Joe, "what's the name and phone number of where you work? Nothing personal, but we need to confirm that. I'm sure you understand."

"Yeah, sure. No problem. Here let me write that down for you." Bunting got up, went to the counter and grabbed a pad and pencil. Giving Joe the sheet with the information on it, Bunting said, "Now I gotta leave. Or I'll be late."

"That's fine, Mr. Bunting. Thanks for your time. Here are our cards in case you think of anything else."

"OK."

The three of them left the house together, Bunting to his car and off to work, and Joe and Ginny to Joe's car and back to the station.

"He doesn't seem a likely suspect," said Ginny. "But I'll call where he works to confirm his alibi."

"I agree. But I'll agree even more fully once you've confirmed his alibi."

Back at the station, Joe and Ginny brought the chief up-to-date with their recent activities and upcoming plans. As usual, the chief's replies were a mixture of grunts, compliments, complaints and encouragement.

Walking back to their desks, Joe said, "Typical chief response."

"Yeah, like beef stew. A little bit of everything. The sooner we solve this case, the better."

"Amen to that."

Joe spent a few minutes calling the parole officers of the two people from the AfA photo-identifications who had given false addresses. Unfortunately, those were the same addresses the parole officers had. They promised to quiz the two men when they were next due for a parole visit, one in two weeks and the other in three.

While Joe was doing that, Ginny checked Bunting's alibi.

When Joe was done, Ginny said, "Joe, I spoke with the

Payroll Department where Bunting works. They confirmed his overtime the Monday evening of Wallerman's death. He worked until 10 p.m. They had his timecard for that week, and it was signed by both his regular supervisor and the night supervisor. Theoretically, he could have made it to Wallerman's house and killed him before midnight, but I have my doubts about him as a killer."

"Me too. So one more for the bottom of our suspect list. By the way, no luck with the two with false addresses. The POs said they'd dig into it when they next see the parolees, one in two weeks and the other in three."

"Joe, gimme a minute to call Mrs. Gould. Then we can start working on the vic's girlfriends or dates or whatever they are."

"OK. I'll grab us some hot coffee in the meantime."

When Joe returned, he gave Ginny her cup and sat down with his cup at his desk across from her.

"All set with Gould?"

"Yes, and some exciting news for you."

"Oh, yeah. This I gotta hear."

"She's a bit unnerved and appreciated my call. She also said she's recently received three more threatening letters related to the sanctuary city stuff she and Wallerman were promoting."

"And the exciting part?"

"We agreed that we'd swing by and pick them up sometime this afternoon."

"Still waiting to hear the exciting part. This just sounds like more possible suspects for us to work through."

"That's true. But the exciting part is that she won't be home this afternoon."

"Huh? What the heck are you talking about?"

"You'll be happy, and I'm assuming excited, to hear that her daughter, Adrianna, will be there all afternoon and she can give us the letters."

"Oh, gimme a break!"

"Just kidding, Joe. I know, you're only a window-shopper. I just couldn't resist."

"Fair enough. You got me this time."

"OK. What say we get started on the girlfriends? Then after lunch we can head over to Gould's house and pick up those letters?"

"Good idea. And maybe we can find a different lunch place in that part of town. Wouldn't mind a change once in a while."

"I assume you're talking about a change for lunch. Not our relationship."

"Correct assumption."

"Let's go into the conference room for this, Joe. It'll help to spread out the names and dates on the whiteboard."

"OK. You bring the phone messages and agenda we got from the vic's paralegal. I'll bring fresh coffee."

"Deal."

As usual, Ginny took her place at the whiteboard, black marker in hand. "OK, we've got nine messages." Ginny quickly looked through them and said, "Five have a first and last name, two a first name and last initial and two just a first name. Fortunately, seven of the nine have a phone number."

Ginny wrote the names or initials and the corresponding phone numbers on the whiteboard. Using the PC in the corner of the conference room and the reverse phone directory, she was able to get the full names and addresses of all nine women. Seven lived in Jasper Creek; the other two lived in nearby towns.

"OK. Let's do a little Googling and Facebooking, as well as checking the DMV and PD files, to learn a little about our new friends."

"Works for me," said Joe. "Why don't you do the Internet stuff and I'll check DMV and our files?"

"OK," said Ginny.

Chapter 27

Two hours later they had both finished going through the names.

"We need to stop now. We'll put our info together later. Time to grab some lunch and head to the councilwoman's house."

"OK. I need a change of pace anyhow. I don't know how you can stare at that computer screen all day. My eyes start to blur and burn after an hour."

"It's probably that age thing again," said Ginny with a smile. "Let me just write 'Do Not Erase' on the board in red so the names and addresses are still here when we get back."

"Good idea. Boy, would I be pissed if it was all erased when we got back here."

Joe and Ginny headed for Gould's house, stopping at a new BBQ restaurant along the way.

After an enjoyable lunch, a sandwich for Ginny and a large, sampler platter for Joe, they were at Gould's house, ringing the doorbell.

"Yes, one moment," could be heard through the door.

A minute later, the door opened and standing there, as attractive as Joe remembered her, was Adrianna Talbot, Elizabeth Gould's daughter.

"Hello, Detectives. My mother said you'd be stopping by. I believe she told you that she'd be out this afternoon."

"Hello, Adrianna," said Ginny. "Yes, your mother told us. We're just stopping by to get some letters she received."

"Yes, come in. Please. It won't take me but a minute to get them."

As Adrianna turned to go get the letters, Joe thought, *No swishing skirt this time. But I'm not disappointed, given the tight tank top and the even tighter pair of short shorts she's wearing.*

Just as Adrianna was returning with the letters, a tall, muscular fellow, who looked to be about 30 years old, came down the steps and joined her at the front door.

"Detectives, this is my husband, Kenneth Talbot. Ken, these are the detectives I told you about who are investigating Councilman Wallerman's death."

"Yeah, I remember."

"Hello, Mr. Talbot," said Ginny as she introduced herself and Joe.

Talbot nodded his response.

Adrianna handed the three letters to Ginny.

"Nice to see you again, Adrianna. And nice to meet you, Mr. Talbot."

Back in the car, Joe asked, "Did you see the husband?"

"Sure did. His tats screamed prison."

"Yeah. And he didn't strike me as overly bright."

"Nor very sociable either."

"You wonder why a put-together girl like Adrianna winds up marrying someone like him."

"Well, you were probably taken at the time. But seriously, I don't know why, but way too many women go for the bad-boy type."

"What a shame. Not surprising to me they're having

marital problems. I just hope, but I'm not too optimistic, that their fighting is only verbal and not physical."

"At least her very short pants clearly demonstrate that he hasn't recently hit her in the legs. No black and blue marks showing."

"I guess so. I hadn't noticed."

"Right. And you probably don't need air to breathe either."

"Very funny. Anyhow, the good news is that there are only three more letters to add to our pile. Damn, we seem to get two or three new potential suspects for every one we eliminate."

"Yup. But this has to turn in our favor sooner or later."

"If I get a vote, I go with sooner."

"Ditto that."

Joe and Ginny were soon back in the conference room at the station.

"OK, Joe, let's finish up with the girlfriends. If we run out of time, we can check Gould's three new letters in the morning."

"OK."

For each of the nine names, in addition to their phone number and address, Ginny wrote on the whiteboard the date of the phone message and what she and Joe had learned: marital status, age, children, work history, where they previously lived, any convictions, and so on. Ginny and Joe were able to also print out photos of eight of the nine, from Google, Facebook or the DMV database.

"Interesting overview, Ginny. The youngest is 24 and the oldest 43. None have any convictions, just miscellaneous driving infractions. Judging from the photos, excluding the few where we only have a DMV photo, and everyone looks ugly in those, they seem to range from pretty to beautiful."

"Why am I not surprised you noticed that?"

"Hey, it's part of my detective-analysis work. And it looks like four of the nine are married, two are single and two are divorced. And we haven't been able to find out anything about the marital state or history of the ninth."

"OK, we've got some visiting to do tomorrow. It may turn out that some of these were calling the vic about legal stuff, but his paralegal didn't get involved, so she doesn't recognize the name."

"Yeah, maybe a few. But I guarantee not all."

"Full agreement."

Pointing to Wallerman's agenda on the table, Ginny said, "OK, let's switch over to his agenda and see which females he's got scheduled for nights or weekends. Or if a few of the phone-message ladies had appointments shortly before or after they called him."

"Let's start by going back six months and see what we get. We can always go back further if we have to."

"OK."

Joe and Ginny quickly realized that this task was close to impossible without Radner's help. There were so many names, some without a last name, and so many that were just initials, Radner's memory and access to Wallerman's files would be essential.

Ginny called Radner. Radner being one of Wallerman's heirs didn't come up during the conversation. Ginny arranged to be at Wallerman's office with Joe at nine the next morning.

"OK, let's call it a day," said Joe. "We can check those three new letters to Gould first thing tomorrow, then head over to the vic's office."

"Sounds like a plan. Joe, if it's OK with you, I could use another quiet night at home."

"Sure. Sounds like a hot bath is more exciting than me."

"Yeah. But just tonight. You're usually much more exciting than a hot bath."

"Wow. That's the nicest thing anyone's said to me all day today."

"Glad I could make your day. Night."

"Have a good one. See you in the morn."

Chapter 28

Ginny was already at her desk when Joe walked in a little past 7:30 the next morning. He was carrying two mugs of coffee.

"Here," said Joe as he handed a cup to Ginny. "I saw your car in the lot so I knew you were here."

"Thanks. How was your night?"

"Good, thanks. And yours?"

"I slept like a baby."

"Oh, sorry to hear that, Ginny."

"Huh? Why?"

"'Cause I care about you. And I'm sorry to hear that you kept wetting your pants and waking up crying."

"Oh, you nutcase," said Ginny as she started laughing. "Anyhow, I had a chance to read the three letters."

"And?"

"We can forget one of them. It was a bunch of ranting and raving against the council's plan to take a corner of Grant's Park and turn it into a dog run."

"Oh. Horrors of horrors."

"The other two are about the sanctuary city proposal. Unfortunately, one of them is anonymous."

"And the other?"

"It's signed 'Your Friends at America for Americans.'"

"That one sounds interesting. What's the letter say?"

Ginny picked it up from her desk. "It's dated five days

ago. 'Dear Councilman Gould: How dumb can you be? Why do you want to protect criminals? We should lock them up or send them back where they came from. We figure this stupidity will end now that your councilman buddy is dead. Guess he won't be protecting any immigrants. Suggest you stop as well. Most sincerely, Your Friends at America for Americans.'"

"Well, that one's clearly to the point. I guess we need to speak with our 'friend at the AfA' again."

"Yes, indeed. We can swing by and visit the fearless leader when we're finished with Radner."

"Good idea. Let's head over to Radner now. The sooner we get started with her, the better."

"OK. Just let me grab the messages and the information we gathered about each caller, along with Wallerman's agenda."

Five minutes later, they were in Ginny's car, on the way to Wallerman's office.

They arrived a half-hour early, but Radner was already there.

"Good morning, Ms. Radner," said Ginny as she and Joe walked into the office.

"Good morning, Detectives."

"Glad to see you're an early riser. OK if we start a bit ahead of schedule?"

"Sure. No problem. I've been getting in extra early the past week or so. It's the least I can do."

"What do you mean?" asked Ginny.

"Oh, I guess you haven't heard. Mr. Wallerman made me one of the heirs of his estate. I can't believe he did that for me. And the amount I'll be getting is unbelievable. A few weeks ago, I was worried about not having a job once this cleanup work is over. Now, I'll never have to work again."

"That's great, Ms. Radner. We're delighted for you."

"It's still horrible that Mr. Wallerman was killed, of course. But I'll never forget what he's done for me. I never expected. . . . OK, enough about me. How can I help you find out who killed him?"

The three of them sat around the table in Wallerman's office. Ginny first showed Radner the information they had assembled about each of the nine callers. Radner carefully reviewed each one and confirmed that the names meant nothing to her and that she knew nothing about any of the women.

Ginny then turned to Wallerman's agenda. "OK, now here's where we really need your help again. We want to go through the last six months with you, page by page. We want to identify every name, or in some cases just initials, that doesn't ring a bell with you. You can help us eliminate most of the appointments, which I'm sure you'll recognize as related to the practice. Of course, a woman client, or a woman lawyer or even a judge could also be one of his female friends. But unless you have any suspicions of any of these, we'll put those aside for now and focus on the ones you don't recognize."

"OK, I'll do my best. It's good that all our files are still here if I need to look at them to be sure. And all the information we have for our billing system will also be useful."

"That's why we came here to do this," said Joe. "Of

course, it may not be helpful if Mr. Wallerman billed the women for his time when he took them on a date."

"Oh, no, Detective. We'd never bill som—"

"I know, Ms. Radner," interrupted Joe. "That was just my poor attempt at a joke."

"Oh, yes, I see that now."

The three of them spent the next two hours meticulously going through the last six months of Wallerman's agenda. The focus was on evening and weekend appointments. Most names were quickly eliminated as Radner recognized them as clients, other lawyers, and investigators whom Wallerman used. Many other names were also quickly eliminated, at least temporarily, if they were obviously male. Others were eliminated, but more slowly. For each of these, Radner checked the corresponding billing information, and in some cases checked to see whether they had a file for that person.

When they were done, they had 15 people, eight with only a first name or with a first and last name, and seven with just initials. Radner confirmed that those with last names were clearly not related to Wallerman's law practice, unless it was a typically non-billed initial meeting with a potential client who decided not to proceed with hiring Wallerman. It was, however, very likely that some or all of these 15 persons were in fact women whom Joe and Ginny would be interested in talking to.

"OK, that's about it," said Joe. "We can let you get back to work now."

"Yes," said Ginny. "We should be able to identify and locate all or almost all of these women using the various databases available to us."

"And then?" asked Radner.

Ginny answered, "Once we identify them and get their addresses, we'll visit them. We'll talk about their relationship with Mr. Wallerman, if and how it ended, any jealous husband or boyfriend in the picture. We'll also ask them if they have any idea who the killer might be."

"Sounds like a lot of work."

"Yes," said Joe. "Too bad it's not as quick and easy as it always is on TV."

"Once again, Ms. Radner, thank you for all your help," said Ginny.

"Oh, you're very welcome. I want to do everything I can to help you find poor Mr. Wallerman's killer."

Chapter 29

J oe and Ginny were soon back in Ginny's car, heading to revisit Frederick Unger, head of the nascent Jasper Creek chapter of the AfA.

"Joe, that was a good session with Radner. We should be able to identify all, or at least most, of the 15 pretty easily once we get back to our desks."

"Yup, especially 'cause my partner's a whiz with her computer."

"Oh, Joe, flattery will get you everywhere."

"That's what I was hoping," said Joe with a chuckle.

"How do you think we should handle Unger?"

"We should enter with both guns blazing. Go at him fast and hard. See if we can knock away some of his composure."

"Works for me."

Ginny pulled partway up Unger's driveway and parked. As they were walking up the rest of the driveway to Unger's cabin, Unger started walking from his cabin to his car.

"Hold on, Mr. Unger. We need to speak with you," yelled Joe as he and Ginny walked up the driveway.

"We already spoke. I'm late for a meeting, so excuse me."

"Your call, sir. We can talk here or we can talk at the station," said Ginny.

"Typical fascist cop stuff! How long will this take?"

"Depends on you," said Joe. "Why don't we step into your house?"

"OK. OK. I guess I don't have much choice. But I'm tellin' you, I'm this close to not talking and calling my lawyer," said Unger as he held up his right hand with his thumb and index finger indicating a very small space between them.

"That's your right. And I'm sure most guilty people would call their lawyer about now."

"I said I'm close to calling, not that I am calling. Yet. OK, come on, let's go inside and get this over with."

Unger led Joe and Ginny into his small, cabin-like house. They sat down around the kitchen table, but Unger wasn't offering any drinks or snacks.

"OK, Detectives. Fire away. The sooner we start, the sooner we're done."

"When did you decide to threaten Mrs. Gould?" asked Ginny.

"What?" No idea what you're talking about."

Joe took the clear plastic folder he was holding and put it on the table between Unger and himself. "Really?"

"What's that?"

"Why don't you take a look at it? We're sure you'll recognize it," said Ginny.

Unger glanced at the letter to Councilwoman Gould.

"Yeah? So?"

"Recognize that letter?" asked Joe.

"Yeah. So what? Nothing illegal about expressing an opinion to an elected official."

"True," said Joe. "Except when it contains a threat. Did you write that letter?"

"Yeah, I did. But it ain't no threat. It just says what we think."

"Referring to the killing of Councilman Wallerman and suggesting that Councilwoman Gould stop promoting that sanctuary city idea sounds like a veiled threat to us."

"Well, you're wrong. You cops are always suspicious about everything."

"Who else did you send a letter like this to?" asked Ginny.

"No one else. Just her."

"Why?"

"Because she and that Wallerman guy were the only two on the town council pushing the sanctuary city idea. The whole idea would probably blow over if those two stopped."

"We know how you stopped Wallerman. And now you're threatening to do the same to Mrs. Gould," said Joe.

"Like I said, it wasn't no threat. Just our opinion."

"Probably not what a jury would conclude," said Joe. "Helped, of course, by the fact that you admitted when we were here last time that you had no real alibi for when Mr. Wallerman was killed. Where's the gun you used?"

"OK. That's it. I'm calling my attorney now."

"No need," said Joe. "We're done and leaving now."

"Just one thing," said Ginny. "For your own good, you better hope nothing happens to Mrs. Gould. You can probably guess who our prime suspect would be."

"You can't scare me. I had nothing to do with Wallerman's death. And if you had any hard evidence, you'd be doing more than just chatting here with me."

"We'll see," said Joe. "Have a nice day."

Joe and Ginny walked back to the car and headed back to the station, stopping at a Burger King along the way for lunch.

Back at their desks, Joe went to bring the chief up-to date, while Ginny began trying to put full names, addresses and any information she could gather to each of the 15 new girlfriend possibilities they now had. The three women whose first and last names they had were easy. Using the phonebook, DMV and PD databases, Google and various social media sites, Ginny had almost a full page of notes for each of the three. She wasn't able to make any progress on the five for whom she had only first names. The seven for whom she had initials were more interesting. It took a little longer than for those whose names she had, but she was able to identify and gather information about four of the seven initials-only women, thanks to the notes in Wallerman's agenda including their phone numbers.

Around three o'clock, Ginny said, "OK, Joe, time to head for our favorite conference room and see where we are with all the girlfriends."

"See how easy it would be with me. I only have one girlfriend."

"Oh, poor you."

"Not to worry. I go for quality rather than quantity."

"Boy, you are quick on your feet today."

With Joe settled into his regular chair in the conference room, Ginny walked up to the whiteboard and starting talking and writing simultaneously.

"OK, Joe. Here we go. We've got nine names from all the vic's phone messages. We were able to identify all nine, and get their addresses and, in most cases, some information about them." Ginny copied the nine names onto the board and put an asterisk next to the two who lived in nearby towns; the other seven all lived in Jasper Creek.

"So far so good," said Joe.

"We didn't do quite so well with the 15 names from earlier today, working with Radner and the vic's agenda. We did identify all three for whom we had first and last names and four of the seven where we only had initials. But we haven't yet identified any of the five where we only have a first name."

"Well, that's still pretty good, given we only got the agenda names and initials earlier today."

"Agreed. And these three," said Ginny as she pointed to three names on the phone message list, "are the same as these three on the agenda list."

"Good. Less work for a pair of weary detectives. Sounds like we know what we'll be doing tomorrow. I better dress nicely to meet all these pretty women."

"Not too nicely, or I'll make sure your nice clothes get all bloody."

"Yikes. Guess I better be careful."

"You betcha."

Joe went down the hall to fill the chief in on their progress in identifying most of these women and to explain that Ginny and he would probably be out all of the next day interviewing them. Ginny started calling the women and was able to reach seven of them and schedule appointments for the next day, either at the women's homes or workplaces.

Shortly thereafter, they both left work and spent the night at Joe's house.

Chapter 30

Their first meeting was with Doris Noonan at 7:30 the next morning. Joe and Ginny drove in Joe's car to Noonan's garden apartment. They parked, quickly located unit 119, walked to the door and rang the bell.

"Good morning. I'm Doris Noonan," said Noonan as she opened the door. "You must be the detectives."

"That's right," said Ginny, after which she introduced herself and Joe.

"Come in. Please. Would you like some coffee?"

Joe and Ginny followed Noonan to the small kitchen at the rear of the apartment, took seats at the table and accepted cups of black coffee.

"Um. Delicious," said Joe. "Be sure you never accept any coffee at a police station."

"Thanks for the warning," said Noonan with a smile. "Sorry we had to meet so early, but I need to leave for work a little before eight."

"Not a problem. We usually start pretty early. Ms. Noonan, as I indicated over the phone, we'd like to talk with you about Mr. Wallerman."

"Yes, for sure. What I shame. But I doubt if I can be of much help. I didn't know Carl, Mr. Wallerman that is, very well."

"Oh?" said Joe. "We understood that you and he dated for a while."

"True. But only if you consider two weeks 'a while.'"

"Why'd it end so quickly?" asked Ginny.

"Darn good question. I have no idea. I thought we were hitting it off well. In fact, I even envisioned that our relationship might get more serious."

"Tell us about it, please."

"Well, it was about four months ago. We met at an art show at one of the local galleries. We left together and had a couple of drinks. He invited me for dinner that Friday night. A very nice restaurant. We had a good time."

"And?" prodded Ginny.

"Uh, well, we wound up spending the weekend at his house. I know what you're thinking. I'm not usually like that. But Mr. Wallerman was very charming, and persuasive, and I was enjoying his company. We had dinner once during the week and then again spent the weekend at his house. He said he'd be very busy for a few weeks, but would call me when things slowed down."

"And did he?" asked Joe.

"Nope. Never heard from him again. I left a couple of voicemail messages on his cellphone and even left one message at his office, but he never called me back."

"Oh," said Ginny.

"Pretty damn rude and inconsiderate, if you ask me. Probably found another vulnerable, but younger, woman to play with."

"You sound bitter," said Joe.

"That's 'cause I am. I feel like he used me and then dumped me to the side of the road."

"Why'd you refer to yourself as vulnerable?"

"I don't think you'd understand. I've been divorced now

for almost four years. I'm OK money-wise, but it's tough meeting decent men. Especially in this small town. And I'm not getting any younger."

"Ms. Noonan, do you know the names of any other women he was dating?"

"No. But I know there were several. Mr. Wallerman was divorced. And as a town council member, as well as having his own law firm, he was viewed as a good catch, if you will."

"Ms. Noonan, do you think your ex-husband might have been jealous about your dating Wallerman?"

"Hah! No way. Even if he knew, which I'm sure he doesn't, he couldn't care less. He married his secretary and they moved to California. I get my alimony check every month, but that's it."

"Ms. Noonan, any idea who might have killed Mr. Wallerman? Or why?"

"No idea. There are probably other women he dumped like me. I was pissed, but surely not to the point of killing him."

"Just so we can cross all the T's and dot all the I's, where were you the evening that he was killed? That would have been Monday, the 23rd of last month."

"That's easy. I was spending that whole week, Sunday to Sunday, with my sister in Massachusetts."

"If you could just give us her name and phone number so that we can confirm that, we're all set."

"Sure. I'll also show you my airline ticket stub and credit card receipts from up there. Just give me a minute."

Noonan left the kitchen. She returned a couple of minutes later and gave Ginny the contact information for her sister and the receipts she mentioned. Ginny and Joe thanked Noonan, gave her their cards and were soon back in Joe's car heading to their next appointment.

"What a shame," said Joe.

"What?"

"The way she's got two inches of makeup piled on her face, and her too-tight blouse. She's clearly having trouble simultaneously fighting her advancing age and finding a husband."

"Jeez, Joe, you're cruel."

"I don't think so. Just honest. How old do you think she is?"

"Not sure. I'd guess mid- to late-40s."

"I agree. Too bad she's trying to look 35."

"Well, in any event, I'll check her alibi. But doesn't sound like she or her ex-husband are prime suspects."

"Full agreement on that, Partner. Let's hope our next appointment's more rewarding."

But it turned out to be even less so. The woman had met with Wallerman one evening to try to get his help in appealing her brother's conviction for burglarizing a house outside Minneapolis. Wallerman explained that he wasn't admitted to the bar outside of Ohio, and therefore couldn't practice law in the Minneapolis area. He checked one of the reference books in his office and gave her the names of two Minneapolis lawyers to call. Joe and Ginny were done with this appointment in 10 minutes.

Having finished so quickly, Joe and Ginny stopped at a Dunkin' Donuts before their next appointment.

They arrived on time for their 9:30 appointment with Mary Boland. The house was small but well kept. It had a very small, neatly mowed front lawn and a red-brick walkway that led to the front door. They were let in, introductions were made and they were soon sitting in the front parlor.

"Ms. Boland," said Ginny, "as I indicated by phone, we'd like to talk with you about your relationship with Mr. Wallerman."

"Yes. But how'd you find out? I thought we kept that very quiet."

"What can you tell us?" asked Joe.

"First off, it's good you're here today. Otherwise, I don't know where we'd meet."

"What's special about today?" asked Ginny.

"My husband left very early this morning with a couple of his buddies to go fishing for the weekend. If he knew about me and Mr. Wallerman, he'd kill me."

"Are you sure he doesn't know?" asked Ginny.

"Oh, definitely. If he knew, you'd be looking either at my dead body or me sitting here all bruised and bleeding. Billy has a lot of good characteristics, but he's super jealous and has a bad temper. Heck, he gets furious if he sees me talking to the boy bagging our groceries at the supermarket."

"Any chance that he did find out and then took it out on Wallerman?"

"No, I'm sure he doesn't know."

"Ms. Boland, how long were you and Mr. Wallerman together?" asked Ginny.

"I wouldn't even call it together. We spent one weekend at his house. That's it. I'm real sorry it happened, but I can't undo it."

"Tell us about it," said Ginny.

"It was another of those weekends that Billy went off with his friends. That time for hunting, not fishing. We had a real fight about it before he left, but that didn't stop Billy.

"I was in Starbucks downtown that next morning. Out of the blue, I started crying like a baby. I couldn't stop myself. Carl was there. He saw me and sat down at my table. He was real sweet, talking with me and trying to get me to calm down. Well, one thing led to another, and we spent the weekend together. I came back here Sunday morning, and that was it."

"Did you have any more contact with him after that?"

"No, that was it. And that was fine. He caught me at a weak moment. End of story."

"Ms. Boland, we're going to have to talk with your husband. That's the only way we can eliminate him as a suspect with certainty."

"My God. Will you have to tell him about Mr. Wallerman and me?"

"Not sure. But most likely. How else can we explain why we're asking him things about Mr. Wallerman's death?" said Joe.

"I understand. But please, please try not to tell him. There'll be hell to pay if he finds out."

"We'll do our best."

As they did with the other women, Joe and Ginny asked Boland where she was at the time of Wallerman's death. She described her weekly Monday night card game with three of her friends, whose names and phone numbers she gave to Ginny.

Joe and Ginny thanked her, said their goodbyes and left for their next appointment. "That husband of hers sounds like a real beauty," said Ginny.

"Yeah. He definitely deserves to meet us. Too bad for her, but she screwed up, literally and figuratively, and will have to pay the price."

"I just hope he doesn't get physical with her."

"Me too. But you did all we could. Suggesting she call the uniformed guys if she feels threatened was the only thing we could do. Maybe when we talk with the husband, we can warn him about abusing her."

"Good idea. That can't hurt, and it may even help."

Joe and Ginny next met with Hikari Saito, an attractive Asian woman who looked to be in her early 40s.

"Ms. Saito?" asked Ginny when Saito opened the door to her apartment.

"Yes?"

"Ms. Saito, I'm Detective Harris and this is Detective McFarland. We're with the Jasper Creek Police Department."

"Oh, yes. You're the one who called me."

"We'd like to speak with you for a few minutes. May we come in?"

"Yes, of course. Please excuse my rudeness."

Ginny noted how Saito spoke without any accent. As Ginny entered the apartment, she stopped when she saw the three pairs of shoes sitting next to the front door. "Ms. Saito, would you like us to take our shoes off?"

"Oh, that would be very nice, if you wouldn't mind. This is an old-fashioned Japanese custom. I don't know why I still follow it. I guess my mother did a good job of drilling it into me when I was a little girl."

Joe and Ginny removed their shoes at the door and followed Saito into the small but attractively furnished living room.

"Would you care for some tea?"

"No. But thank you," said Joe.

"Ms. Saito, your English is perfect. How long have you lived in the U.S.?" asked Ginny.

"Forty-seven years. My whole life. I was born in Camden, New Jersey."

"Oh. Please excuse me. I just incorrectly assum—"

"That's not a problem. Many Caucasians automatically think I was born in Japan. I'm not offended."

"Well, thank you for your graciousness."

"Ms. Saito, as my partner mentioned, we have a few questions, if you don't mind," said Joe.

"Sure. What can I help you with? I know it's about Mr. Wallerman."

"Yes, Ms. Saito, we're investigating his death."

"What a shame. It's been all over the news."

"Ms. Saito, how well did you know him?" asked Ginny. "We know that you had a relationship with him and we'd like to hear more about that."

"Relationship? That's a bit of an overstatement. We met one night in a bar and spent the night together. That's the full extent of what you call our relationship."

"Had you arranged to meet him there?" asked Ginny.

"No. In fact, I never even heard of him before that night. I'm recently divorced, and I just started going to bars, art showings and other events to try to meet men. I tried the online dating thing, but it was terrible. Everyone totally lies about themselves. Some even submit photos that aren't of themselves. After I met a few men from those websites, I decided to try other ways."

"Ms. Saito, can you think of anyone who might want to kill Mr. Wallerman?" asked Joe.

"I have no idea. I really don't know much about him at all. We had a few drinks together in the bar, and then had dinner at an Italian restaurant down the street. I then followed him to his house. We had a couple more drinks, had sex and went to sleep. I left the next morning after we had coffee together. We didn't really spend any time talking, other than about the weather and other superficial things."

"Ms. Saito, how come you only, uh, were with him that one night?" asked Joe.

"It's OK, Detective. You can call it a one-night stand. That's what it was. We both enjoyed the night, but neither of us had any real interest in the other person as a person. Without us saying anything, I knew, and I'm pretty sure he knew, that this was going to be a one-time thing."

"Ms. Saito, just for the record, we need to ask you where you were when Mr. Wallerman was killed. That would have been the evening of Monday, the 23rd of last month."

"Excuse me, please, for one minute. I need to get my calendar from the kitchen."

Saito left the room and quickly returned with a large pin-up calendar in her hand.

"Here it is. I was at a showing at the Cohan Art Gallery. It was from about seven until almost 10. I had hoped to meet some men, but nothing happened. I came home and was in bed by about 11."

"Can anyone corroborate your visit to the gallery that evening?"

"Uh, yes, sure." Saito gave Ginny the name and phone number of one of her girlfriends whom she met at the gallery as well as the name of the gallery manager, who knew Saito from previous showings that she had attended.

Joe and Ginny put their shoes back on, said their goodbyes and headed to their next interview. In the car, Ginny immediately called the two names that Saito had given her.

"OK, Joe. Her alibi checks out. Both people I just spoke to confirm that she was at the gallery until the event ended at about 10 p.m. She still could have gotten to the vic's house and killed him before midnight, but I doubt that she's the killer type."

"I agree with you. One more for the bottom of the suspect list. And another interview that gave us nothing new."

"There was something."

"Oh, what would that be, not to assume foreign-looking people weren't born here?"

"Yes, that is a good lesson. I was pretty embarrassed. But I learned my lesson. But, no, I was thinking of something else."

"Spit it out. I'm all ears."

"Joe, we found Saito from her name in Wallerman's agenda. Right?"

"Yeah. So?"

"Saito said it wasn't a date. She and the vic just met in the bar."

"Right."

"The names in his agenda aren't just for appointments. He didn't have an appointment with Saito. They met by accident. So Wallerman entered her name in his agenda after, not before, their hookup. I didn't think of it until now, but the same thing is true with that Boland woman. He was also using his agenda to record his sexual conquests. Like a scrapbook."

"Jeez, you're right, Ginny. Super observation. What a nutcase he must have been."

"Yeah, or perhaps lonely. Or maybe insecure about getting older and losing some of his sex appeal."

"It's almost like a serial killer sicko, cutting off some hair or a finger as a trophy from each of his victims."

"Correct. But glad we're not dealing with a serial killer in this case."

"Amen to that."

The remaining three interviews that day offered no useful leads. Of the three, two were single and one was married. None of them had any useful information and none stood out to Joe and Ginny as suspects.

Even with a stop for lunch, Joe and Ginny were back at their desks by three. Ginny was able to contact five of the remaining women on their list. She made appointments for Joe and her to meet them on Monday. While Ginny was doing that, Joe printed a copy of Boland's husband's rap sheet. Nothing too serious, but, not surprisingly, there were two misdemeanors for bar fights and one driving license suspension for road rage. The road rage incident also resulted in required attendance at an anger-management course. Joe observed to himself that Boland had probably failed that course.

Joe then got a sudden inspiration and decided to check the rap sheet of the husband of Gould's daughter, Adrianna. Kenneth Talbot was indeed a bad boy. He had spent 18 months as a juvenile in a detention center for breaking and entering. Later, as an adult, he spent 30 months in prison for assault and battery. *Why would a sweet and beautiful girl like Adrianna pick a loser like that?* thought Joe. *She probably could have done better by blindly picking a name out of the phonebook.*

Joe mentioned the two rap sheets to Ginny. They then spent the last 90 minutes or so of the workday checking out the alibis of Noonan, Boland and one of the other women. All the alibis were substantiated.

"OK, Joe. That's it. Time to start the weekend."

Before Joe could answer, his phone rang. Hearing just one side of the conversation, Ginny couldn't decipher much from Joe's "Great." "Super." "That would be fine," and "Thanks again."

"What was that about, Joe?"

"The phone company has the location history for Harkness for the night of the homicide. We can swing by and pick it up on our way home."

"Great. Let's get going. I can't wait to see where he was. And wasn't."

"Me too. It's amazing what technology can do these days."

"Very true."

"Wanna do a Wallerman?"

"What's that?"

"Spend the weekend with me at my house."

"Sure. But only if it doesn't have a Wallerman ending."

"What's that?"

"You dump me and move on to someone else. And then you're killed."

"No need to worry. Your problem will be getting rid of me if you ever want to."

"Fair enough. But I don't see that ever being a problem."

Ginny followed Joe to the phone company. They both parked in the street, almost directly in front of the phone company. Ginny waited in her car while Joe went inside and picked up the location history that was in a large envelope with his name on it at the front desk.

Joe came out of the building, sat in the passenger seat of Ginny's car and ripped open the envelope. He and Ginny rapidly scanned the report.

"Shit," said Joe. "I was really hoping. But, according to this, he wasn't anywhere near Wallerman's house that night."

"Correct. Although technically, all it says is that his phone wasn't. He could have been there without his phone."

"Yeah, I know. It's still possible, but this sure isn't the additional evidence we needed."

"True enough."

"OK, Ginny. There's not much we can do about it. It is what it is. Let's get on with our weekend. Why don't you head over to my place? I'll stop and get some dinner and wine. See you in 30 or so."

"Deal," said Ginny as Joe got out of Ginny's car and into his. They both drove off, Joe to the supermarket and Ginny to Joe's house.

Chapter 31

Joe and Ginny spent the entire weekend doing virtually nothing. Other than driving to a park in a nearby town on Saturday afternoon and taking a long, slow walk in the woods, they basically slept, rested, read, watched TV and ate. They did get into one serious discussion Saturday evening after dinner.

"Joe, this weekend is great. We don't often get to do nothing."

"That's true. And we seem to be pretty good at it. In fact, Ginny, why don't you give up your place and move in here permanently? You're here most nights anyhow. And," said Joe with a grin, "don't think I haven't noticed how your clothes and toiletries are gradually growing in number and overtaking mine."

"Joe, if and when we do move in together, I'd want us to find a new house."

"Why? I thought you liked this place. I mean, it's not a mansion, but it's large enough for the two of us."

"I do like this house. That's not it, Joe. You may think I'm crazy, but I don't want to move into your house. It will always be your house, and I'd feel like the permanent guest."

"Ginny—"

"Let me finish, Joe. Even if my condo were larger, I'd feel your moving into my place would be equally wrong. I'd want us to find a new place. Together. So that, from day one, we'd both be living in *our* house, not yours or mine."

"That is a bit weird, but I can understand it. Really. And I'm OK with it. I don't have any long, lost love for this place. So let's start looking. It might take us a while to find the right place in the right location. And at the right price. Then, when we find it, we can put this place up for sale and, if need be, live in your condo until we close on our new house. And then we could sell your place."

"I'd love to, Joe. But there's another problem."

"What's that?"

"The chief. We're already running a risk, sneaking around together without telling him. Like I learned when I called those other local PDs, the longer the sneaking around, the more likely it was that the chief or the department would force the couple to break up either their relationship or their being partners. And maybe one of them not even being allowed to stay in the department."

"I know. That's why we're being so careful."

"If we were found out now, we could sorta explain that the relationship just started to get serious, we don't know whether it will develop into something more, and so on. But once we buy a house and move in together, that line of fibbing is gone. Hell, we'd even have to give the department the same new address for both of us. That really increases the chances of a negative decision by the chief. It'd even be risky in this small town, where everybody knows everybody else, to start house hunting. "

"Damn."

"What does that mean?"

"It means you're right, Ginny. But I don't like it."

"Well, we agree on that. We're still stuck in our present situation and not knowing what to do. Do we tell the chief and, if so, when?"

"Yup. I say let's solve this Wallerman murder and then tell him."

"What if he won't let us continue as is?"

"We'll figure something out. Look, we both dislike living like fugitives. And not even having committed a crime. We're not going to live like this for the next 25 years until I'm ready to retire. And, like you said, the chief's reaction is more likely to be negative the longer we sneak around before telling him."

"Can't argue with your logic, Joe. But it scares me."

"Me too. OK, let's let it simmer in our heads for a bit and we'll come back at it in a week or so. Now it's time for some butter fudge almond and TV. Chocolate sauce?"

"Yes to the ice cream, but no to the sauce."

"Coming right up."

Chapter 32

Monday morning, their first appointment with one of the remaining woman friends of Wallerman was not until 9:30. She worked the third shift at the local hospital and would be back home and finished with her dinner by then. She was never married, dated Wallerman sporadically over a six-week period, but knew nothing that could help solve the case. The remaining four women had different stories, but were similarly not likely suspects and had no useful information.

On the way to the third woman, Ginny's cellphone rang. It was the one identified woman whom Ginny had been unable to reach, but had left voicemail messages for. It turned out that she had been separated from her husband, but they had recently reconciled. While separated, both she and her husband agreed that they could date other people. She'd spent a few evenings and two nights with Wallerman, after which they mutually agreed to go their separate ways. She was in the process of relocating to Atlanta, where her husband was now working. She'd been in Atlanta for about a month now, and would only be back in Jasper Creek when her house sold so that she could move out all of her belongings. Ginny didn't even bother asking for proof of her alibi or for an alibi for her husband.

"That's it, Joe. We're out of girlfriends whom we've been able to identify."

"We've got more than enough. I'm exhausted just thinking about all Wallerman's dating and sleeping around over a six-month period. Are you sure he was shot and didn't just die from exhaustion?"

"Yup. At least according to the ME. Anyhow, we still have a few alibis to check, but I'm betting they'll all check out."

"Wouldn't be surprised. Let's stop at a McDonalds or Burger King or someplace for a late lunch. I'm starving."

"I'm with you on that."

The weather was sunny and unusually warm. After going into McDonalds to use the restrooms, Joe and Ginny returned to Joe's car and Joe drove to the drive-through window. Eating in the car while parked in a nearby wooded area was a pleasant change.

After eating and while still parked there, Ginny called to speak with Billy Boland. He wasn't home, but his wife was. She told Ginny that her husband was at work and gave Ginny the company's name and address. She also again begged Ginny not to tell her husband about Wallerman. Ginny said they wouldn't if they could avoid it, but they probably would have to tell him. Ginny reiterated her recommendation that Boland call 9-1-1 if she felt at all threatened.

Joe pulled up in front of the garage doors at Premier Body Shop. He and Ginny inquired inside the small glass-enclosed office, and the office manager summoned Boland over the load speaker. A tall, thin and long-haired

Boland came into the office a few minutes later. He held up his greasy hands, making it clear why he and his visitors shouldn't shake hands.

"Billy Boland?" asked Joe.

"Yeah. That's right. And you are?"

"I'm Detective McFarland and this is my partner, Detective Harris," said Joe as he pointed to Ginny. "We're with the JCPD. We'd like to speak with you for a few minutes?"

"About what?"

"Mr. Boland, is there some place private we can speak?" asked Ginny.

"No problem," jumped in the office manager. "I was just heading out to the bank and to run a few other errands. You can stay right here and use my office."

"Fine," said Ginny. "Thank you."

"You're welcome."

Joe sat down behind the desk in the office manager's chair and Ginny and Boland sat in the two visitor chairs in front of the desk."

"OK, what is it?"

"Mr. Boland, what do you know about Carl Wallerman?" asked Joe.

"Who? Nothing. Who is he?"

"He's the town councilman who was killed three weeks ago."

"Oh, yeah. I remember that on TV. Didn't remember the name."

"What do you know about him?" repeated Joe.

"Nothing. Just what was on TV. Someone killed him in his house. Why're you asking me?"

"Your rap sheet says you have a problem with anger."

"Yeah. I used to. But I took a course to solve it."

"And did it work?"

"I'm better than I was. But everybody gets angry some-times. Know what I mean?"

"Yes, I do. But most people's anger doesn't lead to them getting arrested."

"So, what? You're checking out everyone who gets angry to see if they killed that guy?"

"No, not everyone."

"Then why me?"

"Mr. Boland, what do you know about Mr. Wallerman and your wife?" asked Ginny.

"Huh? Whaddaya talking about?"

"Seems like they were playing together while you were out hunting and fishing with your buddies."

"What? No way! Mary would never do that. She wouldn't. She knows I'd kill her if she did."

"Or kill the man she was with?" asked Joe.

"Hell, no. And I didn't mean I'd really kill my wife either. It's just a saying."

"Yes, it is. Where were you when Mr. Wallerman was killed?"

"How the hell should I know? I don't even know when he was killed."

"Three weeks ago today, in the evening," said Ginny.

"Still got no idea. I laid off my social secretary a while ago, so I don't have good records."

"Mr. Boland, you sound like you think this is a joke. Let me assure you it isn't," said Ginny.

"OK, that's it. No more questions without my lawyer with me."

"That's a darn good idea, Mr. Boland. I'm sure we'll talk to you again. Two things before we leave. Don't go outside the county limits without talking to us first. Here are our cards so you can call us," said Joe as he and Ginny each handed Boland a business card.

"Fine. And the second thing?"

Standing up and staring down at Boland, Joe put one hand on the desk, leaned forward and replied, "You better hope your wife stays healthy. If she as much as gets a scratch or a bruise, we'll be all over you. Like white on rice. Understand?"

"Yeah, I gotcha. Can I get back to work now?"

"Sure," said Joe. "Thanks for your time. Have a good day."

Joe and Ginny were in the car heading back to the station.

"Boy, what a bum," said Joe.

"No question."

"I wouldn't put the murder past him if he knew about Wallerman and his wife. But he really did seem surprised when we told him."

"Yes, he did. And I don't think he's smart enough to fake it that well. Joe, I'm going to call his wife to let her know we had to tell him. She won't be happy, but at least she won't be caught off guard when he gets home."

"Good idea. And I meant it. If he so much as touches his wife, he's mine."

"Understood. Let's hope it doesn't get to that."

Joe and Ginny were soon back at their desks.

"OK, Joe. We still have the unidentified girlfriends. From his phone messages, we have one who only left her first name and no phone number. From his agenda, we have five where we just have a first name and three with only two initials. The name from the phone messages could be the same person as one of the initial people on the agenda, but we don't know. So we have either eight or nine unidentified."

"This won't be easy."

"I guess that's why we get paid the big bucks. Let's start with the ones with initials. If they live in town and if they're single and using their own last name, we could find a bunch of possibles by going through the phone book."

"That's a lot of ifs, Ginny."

"Yup. At least it's a start."

"OK, let's do it. We've got NS, AT, and JJ. And the first name we have from the phone messages is Joyce, so that could be our Miss JJ."

Ginny got out the phonebook and started in. She found four females with the initials NS, six with AT and two with JJ, neither of which was a Joyce. She and Joe then checked the names they found against the DMV and PD databases as well as Google and social media sites. Ginny made a note to schedule visits with these 12.

"Joe, before we keep digging, we ought to catch the chief and give him a thorough update before he leaves."

"Good idea."

They entered the chief's office and offered an update of where they were on the case. At the chief's suggestion, they tied in the county prosecutor by phone. It took Joe and Ginny about 15 minutes to get through all the territory they had covered with the hate-mail letter writers, Wallerman's past legal cases, and now his string of so-called girlfriends and their boyfriends or husbands.

"So what are you saying, Detectives? You've worked real hard for three weeks, but still don't know the motive or have any hot suspects. Is that a fair summary?" asked the prosecutor.

"Well, you don't have to make it sound so negative," said Joe. "And, yeah, that's sort of where we are. But, as we described, we do have a couple of very worthwhile suspects."

"You do realize, don't you, that you get paid to solve crimes, not to wear out shoe leather?" the prosecutor insisted.

Leaning forward toward the phone, the chief jumped in. "Hold on, Charles. We understand your frustration. Hell, we feel the same way. And I can guarantee that the mayor's on my ass about this a lot more than he's on yours. Yours'll come once we arrest the perp. Let's not take it all out on Ginny and Joe."

"You're right, Chief. I apologize, Detectives. I just wish we could find the bastard and lock him up."

"So do we. I do think we're making progress," said Joe. "We've eliminated a lot of possible suspects and are digging through the remaining ones we have. We think we're on the right track. We know this wasn't a robbery homicide. And it sure as hell wasn't a suicide. So unless the killing was totally random, or Wallerman was a drug dealer, we've got the most logical probable motives. And we have identified a couple of warm, if not yet hot, suspects. But this stuff takes time. Just as an example, for some of the women he dated, all we have is a first name or a pair of initials. There's no speedy way to convert those to names and addresses."

"Understood. And again, I apologize. Thanks for the update. And please keep at it."

"Don't worry. We will," said Ginny.

After the phone connection ended, Ginny said, "Chief, thanks for jumping in and defending us. We appreciate it."

"Well, that's my job. And when you guys need a kick in the ass, it will be my boot, not the prosecutor's."

"Oh, Chief, you say the sweetest things to us," said Joe with a smile.

"OK. OK. Get outta here and go solve the damn case."

"We will. And, seriously, Chief, we do appreciate your jumping in back there," said Joe.

Back at their desks, Ginny asked, "How about my place tonight for a change?"

"Sure. Happy to oblige. And I vote for pizza."

"Works for me. I'll order a salad with it, and I've got a nice bottle of Chianti waiting for us."

Ginny called and ordered while driving home. The pizza and salad arrived 10 minutes after she and Joe got there. Joe had just finished opening and pouring the wine when the deliveryman rang the bell.

In between bites and sips, Joe and Ginny talked about where they were with the case, and how they needed a lucky break to get to the finish line.

"Boy, this one is tougher than most," said Ginny.

"Yeah. Multiple possible motives. Still a zillion potential suspects even given all we've eliminated. And several with no name or just a first name or initials."

"Not to mention all the possibles who weren't in his agenda or didn't call and leave a phone message. Or didn't write a hate letter."

"Yup, but it could be worse," said Joe.

"Whaddaya mean?"

"How'd you like to be married to that Billy Boland? What a bum. I sure hope he doesn't wind up beating her."

"Me too."

"Or even worse, that piece of crap Councilwoman Gould's daughter is married to. He's an even bigger bum. He actually served hard time. Still can't understand how an attractive and presumably desirable woman winds up with that kind. What's his name again?"

"Something Talbot," said Ginny.

"Oh, yeah, that's right. Maybe his first name is Prisoner."

"Right. Mr. Prisoner Talbot."

"Miss Harris, I'd like to introduce you to this fine couple, Adrianna and Prisoner Talbot. Her mother must be so proud."

"Thank you so much, Mr. McFarland, for the introduction," said Ginny as she bowed deeply in front of Joe.

Joe stood there quietly for a couple of minutes.

"Joe, you all right? You seem deep in thought."

Yeah, I'm fine. I was just thinking. . . . No, forget it."

"Come on, Joe. Let it out."

"OK, but you'll think I'm crazy."

"Won't be the first time."

"I was thinking about our trouble trying to identify the rest of Wallerman's girlfriends."

"And?"

"The initials."

"Yeah? And?"

"There's no way that AT could be Adrianna Talbot, is there? Please tell me no."

"Jeez, Joe. You might be on to something. I'm sure they at least know each other, what with Wallerman and her mother working together on the council. My God, and it's been under our noses all along."

"Let's not get ahead of ourselves. There's nothing under our noses yet. But I think we need to meet with Adrianna and then with Mr. Prisoner Talbot tomorrow morning."

"That's for sure. The earlier the better."

Chapter 33

Joe and Ginny were at their desks around 7:30 the next morning. At eight, Ginny called Gould.

"Hello."

"Hello, Mrs. Gould. This is Detective Harris."

"Oh. Good morning, Detective. Do you have some news?"

"Not yet. But I actually called to speak with your daughter."

"Adrianna? Why? What about?"

"We think she might have some information that might be helpful to us with one of our cases. May I speak with her?"

"Detective, she's not still here. She returned home Saturday morning. Seems she and her husband patched things up. At least for now."

"Glad to hear that. Can you give me her address and phone number?"

"Sure. Happy to."

Gould gave the information to Ginny. They said their goodbyes, and Ginny hung up and called Adrianna's phone number.

"Hello."

"Hello. Is this Adrianna Talbot?"

"Yes, it is. Who's this?"

"Detective Harris. We met at your mother's house a couple of times."

"Yes. I remember. Is everything OK with her?"

"Yes, it is. In fact, I just spoke with her a few minutes ago."

"Oh, that's good. How can I help you?"

"Adrianna, Detective McFarland and I would like to meet with you and ask you a few questions."

"About what?"

"I'd rather not get into it over the phone. Can we swing by and see you this morning? Your mother gave us your address."

"Uh, well. Perhaps we can meet someplace else. My husband doesn't like me having visitors when he's not home, and he's already left for work."

"That would be fine. Where would you like to meet?"

"Um. Let me think for a minute."

"Sure. Take your time."

"I got it. How about the food court at the Platinum Mall? It'll be almost empty until lunchtime."

"Fine. How about we meet at 10:30?"

"OK. I'll see you then."

"Thanks. Bye."

Ginny hung up the phone and said to Joe, "OK. We're set. We'll meet her at the Platinum Mall food court at 10:30."

"OK. Good."

"Yes, but it's a bit weird. Her husband's at work, and he doesn't want her to have anyone at the house when he's not there."

"Weird. Or just plain controlling."

"Could be either."

"The good news is, we'll probably be able to get a decent cup of coffee there."

"Glad you continue to focus on the important things, Joe."

"Just comes naturally to me."

Joe and Ginny left the station around 10. They were sitting in the almost-empty food court when Adrianna arrived just before 10:30.

Adrianna immediately saw the detectives and walked over to them. "Hello."

"Hello," said Joe and Ginny in unison.

"Can I get you a cup of coffee?" asked Joe.

"Thanks. But no. I only have one cup in the morning. And then sometimes another cup at lunch or dinner."

"Sit down, please," said Ginny.

Adrianna sat down on one of the two empty chairs at the table. "What's this about? I've been curious since you called earlier."

"Adrianna," said Ginny, "you know that we've been investigating the death of Councilman Wallerman."

"Yes, of course I do. What a tragedy. Are you close to finding his killer?"

"Not there yet, but making progress," said Joe. "Adrianna, we'd like to ask you a few questions about the councilman."

"Sure. Fine. But I don't know if I can be of any help. I didn't know him all that well."

"How do you know him? And how well?" asked Ginny.

"Basically from town council stuff. I started to go to

some of the meetings when my mom got elected. Over time, I got to meet all the council members."

"Is that all?" asked Ginny.

"Uh, no. I got to know Mr. Wallerman better than most of the others."

"Oh," said Joe as he perked up. "How's that?"

"He and my mom started working together on their sanctuary city proposal. Protecting illegal immigrants and all that. He was at my mom's house several times so the two of them could work on it. And sometimes I was there at my mom's when he came over."

"Is that all?" asked Ginny.

"Mostly. But not all. A few times I dropped off papers for my mom at Mr. Wallerman's office. Oh yeah, and once at his house."

"Adrianna," said Joe. "How would you describe your relationship with him?"

"What do you mean?"

"Adrianna, it's not a trick question. Did you barely know him? Or did you know him well? Did you become friends? Good friends? That sort of thing."

"Well, I guess I'd say someplace between barely knew him and knew him fairly well. Definitely not friends."

"Adrianna, the truth. How often did you have sex with him?" asked Joe.

"What? What are you saying?" said Adrianna loudly.

"You might want to keep it down. This place is pretty empty, but there are some other people here."

"Yes. You're right. Thank you."

"Adrianna, you haven't answered my question," said Joe.

"Never. How can you even think that?"

"Adrianna, I'm going to ask you that question once more, but first I want to tell you three things. First, lying to a police officer who is investigating a crime is itself a crime. Second, you have the right to stop talking with us until you have a lawyer at your side. And, probably most importantly, we know about you and Mr. Wallerman. We have definitive evidence of your relationship with Mr. Wallerman. It will go easier for you if you voluntarily tell us everything."

"What are you implying? Am I a suspect? Do you think I killed him?"

"No, you're not a suspect," said Ginny. "We don't think you're the killer."

"Then why are you badgering me about this?"

"Let's stick to where we're the ones asking the questions," said Joe. "So, OK, now, how long had your affair with Mr. Wallerman been going on?"

"There is no affair and never was one."

"Adrianna!" said Joe. "We have the proof. This is the last time I'm asking before we take a trip to the station. How often did you have sex with him?"

All of a sudden, Adrianna started crying. She took a tissue, and then a second one out of her handbag. She almost had her crying under control a couple of times, but then the tears and hard crying returned. Joe and Ginny just sat there silently and waited.

In between sobs, Adrianna mumbled something that sounded like "un."

"What did you say?" asked Ginny.

"One. Just one time."

"Tell us about it," said Ginny.

"Not much to tell. I made a stupid mistake. Once. That was it. I swear."

"When was this? And where?" asked Joe.

"It was almost two months ago. At my mother's house. In my old bedroom, which my mom now uses as a guest room."

"Was your mother home?" asked Joe.

"My God! No! What do you think I am? My mom was in Dayton, meeting with a client of her Internet business, and it was about three in the afternoon."

"And?" prodded Joe.

"Mr. Wallerman brought some papers over for my mother. He figured no one would be home and he'd leave them under the front door mat. But he knocked, and was surprised when I answered the door. I was staying at my mom's for a few days. Ken and I had had a big fight. Just like the one we had a couple of weeks ago. Only bigger."

"Tell us what happened with Mr. Wallerman," said Ginny.

"Well, I was just trying to be nice. So I invited him in for a cup of coffee."

"And?"

"I don't even know how it happened. We were just talking. And he asked me how come I was there at my mom's house. I explained how I was recently laid off from my job as a bookkeeper at a small construction company 'cause they were having a temporary slowdown in their business. Then I started explaining that I was staying at my mom's house for a few days because my husband and I had a big fight. Then, before I know it, I'm bawling like a baby. Sobbing just like I did a few minutes ago. I don't know, I just can't seem to control it anymore."

"Then what happened?" asked Ginny.

"Mr. Wallerman started trying to comfort me. I don't even know what he was saying. Then he moved his chair next to mine. I wound up with my head on his shoulder and his arms around me. I still can't figure out what happened next. Before I knew it, we were kissing and other stuff. And I was enjoying it and getting aroused. I think it was more a reaction to how Ken was treating, or, I should say, mistreating me. Before I knew it, we were upstairs on my old bed taking our clothes off. Then we did it. It was over quick. I didn't really enjoy it, and I was sorry and ashamed as soon as we were finished. We got dressed, Mr. Wallerman left and that was it."

"And since then?" asked Joe.

"I saw him a couple of times. But never alone. I was always with my mother. Neither he nor I ever mentioned it to each other or tried to do it again, or anything like that."

"Adrianna, when did your husband find out?"

"What! He doesn't know about this. Does he? If he ever found out he'd kill me or. . . . My God, you don't think Ken killed Mr. Wallerman? Do you?"

"We don't know. What do you think?" asked Ginny.

"No. He's tough, especially with me, but he'd never kill anybody."

"Adrianna, does your husband own a gun?"

"Yeah, sort of. Several. He's always going hunting."

"What do you mean by sort of?" asked Joe.

"Officially, I bought them. They're in my name. Ken can't legally buy or own, or even use, a gun, because he's a convicted felon."

"Do you know what kind of guns?"

"No, I don't. I'm not really a gun person. I know that most are rifles. At least one is a handgun or a pistol or whatever you call it."

"Adrianna, can we go to your house with you and look at his guns? Just to be sure."

"I'm afraid. If I let you do that and Ken found out, he's like to almost kill me. Can't you ask him yourself?"

"Yes, we can. Just thought this would be easier and quicker," said Joe.

"I understand. But, please. I'd rather you ask him. And, please, don't tell him about Wallerman and me, whatever you do. And don't tell him I told you about the guns. Please!"

"We won't unless we have to at some point. Where does he work?"

"Atlas Molding. Over on 13th."

"I know where that is," said Joe.

"That's it for now, Adrianna. Thanks for your time. And your honesty."

"Yeah. Sure."

And with that, all three left the mall and got into their cars, Adrianna to head back home, and Joe and Ginny back to the station. After parking at the PD, Joe and Ginny walked around the corner for their normal lunch at Sancho's Taco Shop.

"Well, Joe. I think we finally have a hot lead."

"So do I. If Talbot found out about Adrianna and our vic, he'd be a very strong suspect in my book."

"Yup. That'd be plenty of motive. Not to mention his guns and his past violent crime conviction."

"We've got to find out if he knows, and when he found out if he does. And then we've got to check out what handguns he has."

"In fact, Joe, let's not even go back to our desks. Let's finish our lunch and go see Talbot now."

"Good idea, Partner."

Chapter 34

Forty-five minutes later, Joe pulled up in front of Atlas Molding. It was a large, two-story, tan brick building that looked like it had been there since the Industrial Revolution. The lower level windows all had metal bars on them. What was obviously the office area appeared to be a small one-story more modern section that had been added to the front of the building.

Joe and Ginny walked up the badly cracked, concrete walkway and entered the office. They walked to the unoccupied reception desk. There was a small, grease-smudged sign next to the telephone that said, "Visitors. Please dial 0."

Joe picked up the phone and dialed "0." He heard the phone ring, but no one answered. Two minutes later, a slightly plump woman, probably in her mid-50s, walked out from a door in the corner of the room.

"Hi. I'm Alice. Welcome to Atlas Molding. How can I help you?"

"Hello," said Ginny. "We're with the Jasper Creek Police Department, and we'd like to speak with one of your employees."

"Uh. Yeah. Sure. Who?"

"Kenneth Talbot."

"Hold on. Let me check." And then a minute later after she did her thing with the PC on the receptionist's desk, "Yes, he's in today. In fact, he's most likely still in the breakroom having lunch. His lunch period ends in about 10 minutes."

"Fine. Can you take us to him?" asked Joe.

"Sure. No problem. Follow me."

Following Alice into the breakroom, Joe and Ginny immediately recognized Talbot sitting alone at one of the tables in the last row against the back wall.

"OK. We see him. Thanks," said Joe.

"You're welcome," said Alice. But she stood there watching as Joe and Ginny walked to Talbot, positioning themselves on either side of him.

"Mr. Talbot. Remember us?" asked Joe.

"Yeah. What's up?"

"We'd like to talk to you for a few minutes," said Ginny.

"About what?" asked Talbot.

"Not here. Is there someplace we can talk?"

"Uh, I think so. Let's go."

Talbot got up, left his mostly finished lunch on the table and walked toward the door. Joe and Ginny followed.

"Hey, Alice. Can we use the training room for a few minutes?"

"No problem. It's not reserved at all today."

"Thanks," said Talbot.

"Thank you," Ginny said to Alice. Joe gave her a friendly nod.

Joe and Ginny followed Talbot out of the breakroom and into the training room almost directly across the hall. All three sat down around a rectangular table large enough to hold eight people.

"OK. So what's this about?"

"Mr. Wallerman," said Joe.

"Who?"

"Town Councilman Wallerman," said Ginny.

"Oh. You mean that politician who was murdered?"

"Yes. That's the one."

"What about him? I never met him."

"Are you sure?"

"Yeah, I'm sure. But what difference?"

"We're investigating his murder," said Joe.

"That's good. Ain't that what the cops are supposed to do?"

"Yes, it is. And we're doing it."

"Good for you. But what's that got to do with me?"

"Mr. Talbot, where were you when he was killed?"

"Why you asking me that?"

"Mr. Talbot, if you don't mind, we'd like to be the one asking the questions," said Joe.

"Just because I'm an ex-con, it doesn't mean I killed him. Or anybody. Hell, there are a lot of other ex-cons around here. Maybe one of them killed him."

"Yes, maybe," said Ginny. "But please answer our question. Where were you when he was killed?"

"How the hell do I know? I don't even know when he was killed."

"It was Monday, the 23rd of last month. Between eight and midnight."

"I'm sure I was home. We don't go out much during the week."

"Were you alone? Can anyone corroborate that?" asked Joe.

"Yeah. I'm sure my wife was with me. Why? You really think I killed that guy?"

"Mr. Talbot. Your wife wasn't with you. She was actually staying with her mother for a few days."

"What? How do you know where my wife was staying when?"

"We're detectives, Mr. Talbot. That's what we do," said Ginny.

"Well, then, if you're so sure, I guess I was alone at home. I'm not big on entertaining."

"Do you own guns?"

"Doesn't everyone hereabouts?"

"Yes, quite a few do."

"Like a lot of folks, I like to hunt."

"What kind of guns do you have?" asked Joe.

"A Winchester 70, a Marlin .338 and a Remington 870 shotgun. But they're not mine."

"What do you mean?" asked Joe.

"Very cute. Nice try. You know damn well that a felon like me can't own a gun. And I don't. They're actually owned by wife."

"Oh, and you just borrow them?" asked Ginny.

"I never said that. I said I like to hunt. I didn't say I do hunt."

"Don't sweat it, Mr. Talbot. We're not here on behalf of the ATF."

"Yeah, well, I don't know why you're here."

"How about handguns? Do you, or should I say your wife, own any?"

"Just one."

"Are you sure?" asked Joe.

"Yup."

"What make and model?"

"I can't remember."

"I bet. Mr. Talbot, would it be all right if we searched your home to see the guns?"

"Sure. No problem at all. All you need is a search warrant."

"OK. If that's how you want to play it. Something to hide?"

"Nope. Just exercising my rights."

"Fair enough. We'll get a warrant easy enough," said Ginny. "In the meantime, we'd like you to come back with us to the station for some more questioning."

"But what about my job here? I can't just walk out."

"Don't worry," said Ginny. "We'll write you a note explaining your absence."

"And if I refuse to come with you?"

"You'll be in big trouble," said Joe.

"I don't think so. I'm not as naïve as you think. Unless you're arresting me, I don't have to go with you or answer any of your questions."

"No, that's right. You don't have to," said Joe. "But that will clearly raise suspicions about your innocence."

"Seems like you already have those suspicions. So, unless you're arresting me, I'm done talking with you and I'm not going with you."

"That's your right. We'll see you soon with that search warrant. And don't be concerned when you see a police-man following you around. We'll be arranging that to be sure you don't try to toss any guns you may have."

"Sounds like harassment to me. Just because I'm an ex-con."

"I don't think so," said Joe. "But you can check with your lawyer. In any event, we'll see you again soon."

"Thrilling. I can't wait."

While driving back to the station, Ginny called Prosecutor Porter and arranged for a meeting as soon as she and Joe could get there. Ginny explained that they had a hot suspect and wanted to search his house and car for a handgun that they could then have ballistics test. But they needed to do the search quickly before the suspect got rid of the gun they assumed he had. She then called Patrol and requested a dedicated tail on Talbot until they obtained and executed the search warrant, with a focus on ensuring he didn't discard a gun in the river, a garbage can, in the brush alongside a highway or anywhere else.

Chapter 35

Joe and Ginny were soon sitting in Porter's office.

"OK, Detectives. Whaddaya have and whaddaya need?"

"A hot suspect. And a search warrant," said Joe.

"Very cute. How about a little more detail on each?"

Joe and Ginny brought Porter up to date on their investigation, including Adrianna's sexual encounter with the vic and their suspicion that her husband might be the killer. They explained his violent criminal past and his admitting to having rifles and one handgun in the house. They explained that they wanted to search his house and car to see if they could find one or more handguns, specifically the one used to kill the victim.

"Sounds reasonable. I should be able to get you the warrant."

"Great. And not to be greedy, but the faster the better. We've already talked to the suspect, including asking him if he had any handguns. He refused to let us search his house without a warrant, and he knows we'll be trying to get one. We're concerned that if he has the murder weapon, he'll dump it before we can conduct the search. We've got the uniforms watching him, but that's a lot less than foolproof."

"Understood. Give me his name and address, and the make and model of his car, and I'll get to work."

Joe and Ginny gave Porter the requested information.

"OK. One question before I get started. Any other locations you want to include? It's tougher to come back later and add additional locations. The judges tend to view that as fishing expeditions."

"Like what other locations?" asked Joe.

"Is there an unattached garage? Or a barn? Or a garden shed? Those're different than the house if they're not attached to it. Or does his wife have a second car? Does he have a hunting blind? How about his locker or desk at his place of employment? I can keep going. Is this enough?"

"Yes. We get the idea. His wife does have her own car, and we should include that."

"Their garage is attached to the house and there're no freestanding other buildings on the lot. No idea about a hunting blind, but I'd doubt it," said Joe.

"But let's add his locker at work. Just to be sure. It can't hurt," added Ginny.

"OK. Is that it now?"

"Yup. I think so," said Joe.

"Joe, do you think we should add Adrianna's mother's house? The daughter's often there, and he's there occasionally. I wouldn't put it past him to hide the gun there."

"Good point, Ginny. Yeah, Charles, let's add that."

"Hold on. Now it's getting a little dicey. It was bad enough when the son-in-law of a councilwoman is your prime suspect. Now you want to also add her house to the search warrant. You do know that I have to work with these people."

"Yes, we know. But when you get the warrant, maybe you, or us if you prefer, can tell Councilwoman Gould that her house is included because of her son-in-law. It's not that we suspect her of anything."

"How about we leave her house off this warrant? If you don't find anything at the other locations, we can ask Mrs. Gould if she'll allow us to search her house for a gun. Presumably she'll agree, and then you can search her house thoroughly without a warrant."

"Works for me," said Ginny.

"Me too," said Joe.

"OK, get outta here now. Let me look up the info on the wife's car and then get to work on this with one of our friendly judges. I'll call you when I have the warrant. Shouldn't be more than a couple of hours."

"Great. Thanks," said Ginny.

Joe gave Porter the address of Talbot's employer, then he and Ginny left Porter's office and walked back to the station to wait for his call. Joe walked down to the Patrol sergeant to alert him to the likely need for a few officers to help with a search that evening.

Porter called around 5:30. "OK, I've got the warrant. Faxing it to you now."

"Great. Thanks for the speedy service."

"My pleasure. Hope it gets us our perp."

"We're giving it our best shot. We're off to conduct the search now."

Joe, Ginny and three uniformed officers showed up at the Talbots' house about 40 minutes later. After showing the search warrant to a surprised Adrianna and an angry Ken Talbot, the police spent about 2½ hours going through the house and two cars neatly but very thoroughly. They saw the rifles that Talbot had admitted to, but found no handguns. They found several boxes of ammunition in the bottom drawer of an old dresser in the bedroom. Most of the ammunition was for the three rifles, but there was one box of 10mm ammunition, clearly for a handgun rather than a rifle. Since ammunition wasn't explicitly listed in the search warrant, they couldn't seize it as evidence and could never use its existence as evidence in court. Nonetheless, it did further convince Joe and Ginny that there surely is, or was, a 10mm handgun someplace. Even though they were unsuccessful at finding it.

Shortly before nine, Joe and Ginny thanked the Talbots for their cooperation, and all the police left. Joe and Ginny were starved. They stopped at the first place they could, a Wendy's, for a quick dinner: two double hamburgers for Joe and one large Bacon Deluxe burger for Ginny, with fries and Diet Cokes for both.

"The burgers taste fine," said Joe. "But I'm still not a big fan."

"Why?"

"I don't know. It must have been something in my childhood, but square hamburgers are weird."

"Yes, they are. Especially on round rolls. Anyhow, more to the point, whaddaya think about our search?"

"We clearly were thorough. So that gun is not there."

"Yeah. But the ammo sure tells us there's a 10mm handgun someplace."

"Well, first thing tomorrow, as soon as they're open, we should present the warrant to his employer and search his locker. Maybe the gun's there."

"Yeah, maybe. But that seems like too obvious a place to hide it. He's dumb but not that dumb."

"Probably right, Ginny. But we'll know for sure tomorrow."

"Yup."

Joe and Ginny finished dinner, headed to Joe's house and enjoyed a good night's sleep.

Chapter 36

Joe and Ginny were at Atlas Molding at 7:15 the next morning. They were waiting at Talbot's locker when he arrived just before 7:30.

"You again?"

"'Fraid so. This warrant," said Joe as he waved the warrant in the air, "allows us to search your locker. Please open the lock."

"And if I don't?"

"I'll go get the bolt cutter from my trunk and cut the lock off," said Joe.

"OK. OK. No need. Here you go."

Talbot unlocked his locker. Ginny had him stand back while Joe opened the locker and searched it. As the locker was small and virtually empty, the search took all of 10 seconds.

"OK. Happy now?"

"Sure. It's a nice sunny morning. Why wouldn't we be happy? Especially since we'd like you to come downtown with us for a few more questions."

"And why would I do that? I know my rights. I don't have to go with you unless you have a warrant or are arresting me."

"Very good, Mr. Talbot. Perhaps you should have become a lawyer. You probably also know that it's illegal for a felon to be in close proximity to a gun, even if it's owned by someone else, like their wife. And, add to that the fact that's it's our choice whether or not to inform ATF."

"That's blackmail!"

"No, sir. It's merely informing you of your options and the ramifications of what you choose."

"OK. OK. I'll go with you. But I don't know how many questions I'll answer without a lawyer."

"That's your right," said Ginny.

"What about my job? I can't just walk off."

"We'll stop at the office on the way out and explain that we need your help for a few hours. I'm sure they'll let you go with us."

They stopped in the office. Ginny explained just that to the office manager, who said she'd note the approved few hours off in Talbot's file. Joe and Ginny thanked the office manager, and the three of them left.

Once back at the station, Joe and Ginny sat with Talbot in one of the interrogation rooms. Joe turned on the recorder, and specified the date, time, location and who was in the room. He then read Talbot his Miranda rights.

"Yeah. I understand all that crap. But it don't matter cuz I didn't kill that guy."

"When was the last time you saw Mr. Wallerman?" asked Ginny.

"Never. I told you, I didn't even know who he was."

"But you do agree you have no alibi for when he was killed?"

"Yeah. But that's probably true for millions of people. Why you looking at me? Just because I'm an ex-con?"

"In part," said Joe.

"What else?"

"Your indirect relationship with Mr. Wallerman."

"What the hell does that mean?"

"Mr. Talbot, why was your wife staying at her mother's house the night of the murder?" asked Ginny.

"'Cause we had a fight and she went there for a few days. But what's that got to do with any of this?"

"What was the fight about, Mr. Talbot?"

"None of your damn business. That's personal."

"Sorry," said Ginny, "but we happen to think it's very relevant. So tell us."

"OK, if you must know. I found out the whore was cheating on me."

"With whom?" asked Ginny. "Anyone we've been talking about here?"

"Jeez! You guys snoop into everything. Yeah, it was that Wallerman guy."

"How'd you find out?" asked Joe.

"My tramp of a wife just up and told me. Like she apologized and thought I'd forgive and forget. Fat chance!"

"Mr. Talbot, is that why you shot Mr. Wallerman?"

"No way. If I shot anybody, it woulda been my so-called loyal wife. She's the one that swore vows to me. That Wallerman guy didn't. Hell, he was just doing what any man would do. It's in our genes, you know."

"And your wife?"

"She shoulda learned how to keep her legs closed. Decent women don't do that kinda thing. Except, of course, with their husband. I hadda go marry one of the bad ones."

"Mr. Talbot, what about the—?"

"Stop. Hold it. That's it. I'm done. Either arrest me, or I'm leaving."

"That's your right," said Joe. "We're not arresting you. Yet. But don't leave town. I'll walk you downstairs and arrange for one of the patrol cars to take you back to work."

"Thank you so much for coming in, Mr. Talbot. I'm sure we'll be seeing you again shortly," said Ginny in her sweetest voice.

Joe walked Talbot downstairs and arranged for his ride. Joe and Ginny then met back at their desks.

Joe's first sentence was "Damn!"

"I agree. But it's what we both expected."

"Yeah. I know. But a pleasant surprise would've been appreciated. It woulda been so nice if he just confessed."

"Joe, we both have a feeling about this. He's a real piece of work. Now we need some hard evidence."

"Agreed."

Chapter 37

"I guess our next step should be Gould's house. Let me just call Porter and double-check that he's still fine with us just asking her if we can search her house."

Ginny called Porter and he confirmed that their talking with Gould would be fine with him.

Joe and Ginny pulled up in front of Gould's house at about 8:30. They walked to the front door and rang the bell.

Opening the door, Gould said, "Oh, hello, Detectives. Any news? Glad you caught me. I was about to head out for a few errands."

Ginny explained why they were there. Gould was not surprised as Adrianna had called her earlier that morning to tell her about the search done the prior evening.

"I'm not Kenneth's biggest fan, and was dead set against Adrianna marrying him. But I really doubt that he's a killer. And of Carl. What would be his motive? They barely knew each other."

"I'm afraid you'd have to ask Mr. Talbot, or perhaps your daughter, about that. As you know, we searched their house and cars last evening, but didn't find any handguns. So we'd like your permission to search your house," said Joe.

"My house? Why? Surely you don't think I—"

"No, not at all," interrupted Ginny. "But Mr. Talbot's

here sometimes, and he might have hidden the murder weapon someplace here."

"I don't even want to think about that. I'm OK with you searching, but before I officially say yes, I'd like to check with my attorney. Just to be sure. Hope that's not a problem."

"No, that's fine."

"I'm sure there's no gun here. Ken does come occasionally, but it's been less and less recently. Plus, I or Adrianna or both of us have been here whenever he's here. And he's rarely alone to roam the house to hide something. And with all the cleaning and rearranging of things I'm always doing, I think I would have come across the gun if he'd hid it here."

"Well, as you can imagine, we need to check for ourselves just to be sure. If you could get back to us later today after you speak with your lawyer, we'd appreciate it. We'll get out of your hair now so you can take care of your errands. I know I gave you my card earlier, but here's another one so you don't have to spend time searching for it."

"OK. Thanks. I'll call as soon as I talk with my attorney."

"Fine. Thank you, Mrs. Gould."

Joe and Ginny were back in their car.

Joe said, "Nice woman. I hate the delay, but I understand her wanting to check with her lawyer first."

"Yes. It's actually the smart thing to do. I'm guessing she's worried an awful lot more about her daughter than her son-in-law."

"I'm sure you're right about that. While we're waiting to hear back from Mrs. Gould, let's swing by Adrianna's house again. I'd like to question her about any handguns without her husband being there," said Joe.

"Good Idea."

Chapter 38

"Huh. Oh, hello, Detectives," Adrianna said after answering the doorbell.

"Hello, Adrianna," said Ginny. "We have a few questions. May we come in?"

"Uh, yes, I guess so. But we need to make this quick. I told you that my husband doesn't like me to have people in the house when he's not here."

"This will only take a very few minutes."

"Fine. Come in."

Joe and Ginny were soon sitting in Adrianna's kitchen.

"Adrianna," said Ginny. "We want to ask you specifically about any handguns you or your husband have."

"Yes, we do have one. Like the rifles, Ken had me buy it in my name because of his record."

"May we see the gun?" asked Ginny.

"Sure. But it's not here."

"Oh," said Joe.

"I took it to my mother's."

"When? Why? Tell us the whole story, please," said Ginny.

"Well, after my, um, thing with Mr. Wallerman, I was getting more and more upset with myself for letting it happen. And I was feeling terrible having cheated on Ken like that. He's got a lot of faults, but I don't think he ever cheated on me. I didn't tell you the truth when we met at the mall yesterday. Ken did know about it. Four or five days after Mr. Wallerman and I uh, you know, did it, my guilt got so bad I decided to tell Ken and ask for his forgiveness."

"And did you?"

"Yeah, but it was a mistake. I expected he'd be mad and upset, but I hoped he'd soon calm down and forgive me. But, boy, was I wrong. We had our worst fight ever. It lasted for days. And he called me every name in the book. Tramp. Slut. Whore. And a bunch of other things I won't even repeat."

"Did he hit you?" asked Joe.

"Not really hit, but he did a lot of squeezing and shaking. And he pushed me against the wall a few times. He said he'd like to kill me. Or at least cut me all up with his hunting knife. I was really scared."

"What happened next?" asked Ginny.

"The next day, after he left for work, I packed a few things and went to stay at my mom's for a while. I was scared enough that I took that handgun with me so that my mom could hide it until Ken calmed down. I figured if he was going to come after me, he'd more likely use that than one of his rifles. Plus, he used his rifles much more than his gun for hunting, so I hoped he wouldn't notice the gun was missing."

"And what happened next?" asked Joe.

"When I got to my mother's, I wound up telling her the whole story. About Mr. Wallerman. And Ken. And I gave her the gun to keep at her house for a while."

"What was your mother's reaction?" asked Ginny.

"She, of course, was very upset. And worried about me.

She complained a bit about Ken, but a lot more about Mr. Wallerman. She was irate at what he'd done to me. She said it wasn't my fault, that he took total advantage of me. She was really furious."

"Do you know where she put the gun?" asked Joe.

"No. She just said it's in a safe place until Ken eventually calms down."

"OK," said Joe. "Thanks for your help. We're going to be heading out, but first we're going to arrange for a police officer to spend the next few hours with you."

"What? Why?"

"Adrianna, it's just a formality. We need to ensure, for the record, that you don't now speak with your husband, or your mother or anyone else for the next few hours."

"Why? Do you think I'm the murderer?"

"No," said Ginny. "But we'll be speaking with these and other people shortly and we need to avoid any possible suspicion that you told them about our conversation before we speak with them."

"Ginny, wanna call Patrol and have them send their closest uniform here?"

"Sure."

Ginny made the call, and 10 minutes later, Officer Bill Stanton arrived. Introductions were made, Ginny apologized to Adrianna for any inconvenience, and Joe explained to the patrolman that his responsibility was to not let Adrianna make or receive any phone calls. Joe and Ginny wrapped up the conversation, thanked Adrianna and headed back to the station, leaving Adrianna and Officer Stanton standing in the foyer.

Chapter 39

Joe and Ginny had just returned to their desks when Gould called.

"Hello. Detective Harris speaking."

"Hello, Detective. This is Elizabeth Gould. I just hung up from talking with my attorney."

"Great. Thanks for calling so promptly. So, what did he say?"

"He agreed that there's no problem you searching for the gun. I'm still out running around. I'll be home in about an hour and then expect to be there the rest of the day. So whatever time works for you would be fine."

"Good. Thanks. How about we stop by right after lunch? Say about 1:30."

"Fine. I'll see you then."

Joe called the Patrol sergeant and arranged for two patrol officers to meet Ginny and him at Gould's house at 1:30 to assist with the search.

Joe and Ginny grabbed lunch at Sancho's and were at Gould's house at 1:20. Gould opened the door and let them in almost immediately after Joe rang the doorbell.

"Come in, Detectives."

"Thank you," said Ginny as she and Joe walked through the door. "We suggest you pick one room and stay in it while we search your house. We'll be thorough, but we'll be as quick and neat as we can."

The front doorbell rang. When Gould opened it, two uniformed cops were standing there. They introduced themselves and entered the house and said hello to Joe and Ginny.

"OK. Have at it. I'll be in my home office, off the kitchen, doing some work."

"Fine. Thanks. Before we start our search," said Joe, "any ideas where your son-in-law might have hidden the gun? We'll search those areas first. Maybe we'll get lucky."

"Sorry. I can't help you there. As I told you this morning, I can't believe there's a gun hidden here. And if Ken did hide it here, I have no idea where."

"OK," said Joe. Then turning to the two uniformed officers, "Why don't you two start down here. We'll take the upstairs."

"Will do."

With that, Joe and Ginny started up the stairs, the two officers went into the living room and Gould walked back into her home office.

Joe and Ginny began in the master bedroom and adjoining bathroom. They found nothing. They then moved down the hall to Adrianna's former bedroom. It took them only about five minutes to find a Glock 40 pistol, along with two clips, under a pile of T-shirts in the bottom drawer of the dresser standing opposite the bed. Using her gloved hands, Ginny put the gun and two clips in a plastic pouch, sealed it, and wrote the date, time, and location found on the plastic bag. She then signed her name on the bag.

They walked back downstairs. Ginny showed the gun

and clips to the two officers who had finished searching the living room and were on their way to begin in the kitchen. Joe and Ginny walked into Gould's office.

"I'm sure you're as surprised as we are, but look what we found," said Joe as Ginny held up the plastic bag.

"Oh, my goodness," said Gould. "I can't believe it. Where'd you find it?"

"In the dresser in your guest room, what I assume was Adrianna's old bedroom," said Ginny.

"That damn Kenneth! How could he do such a thing? Killing Carl and then trying to make it look like Adrianna, or even me, is the one that did it. I'm glad you caught him. I hope he rots in hell, or at least in prison."

"Mrs. Gould, we need you to come downtown with us. We need to ask you a bunch of questions so we can document exactly what happened."

"It'd be my pleasure. I'm ready whenever you are."

Chapter 40

Five minutes later, Joe and Ginny were driving back to the station, with Gould sitting in the back seat. Ginny took Gould into one of the two interrogation rooms. She gave Gould a bottle of water and said that she and Joe would be back in about 10 minutes to begin. While Joe was bringing the chief up to date and inviting him to witness the interrogation, Ginny did the same by phone with Prosecutor Porter.

Fifteen minutes later, Joe and Ginny walked back into the interrogation room, with Ginny carrying a tape recorder and a notepad with two pencils. The chief and prosecutor were standing outside the one-way mirrored window, ready to watch the interrogation. They were also able to hear it through the speaker hanging on the side wall.

"Ready?" asked Ginny as she and Joe sat down.

Ginny spent the first minute or two speaking into the recorder, stating the date, time and location and identifying the three people in the room. "OK, Mrs. Gould. Are you ready to begin?"

"Yes. Do you think I should ask my lawyer to join us?"

"That's totally up to you. You, of course, are entitled to do so if you wish."

"Um, I think I should. I've got nothing to worry about, of course, but I've always been advised not to do things like this without a lawyer."

"Fine. Why don't you call him now?"

Gould took her cellphone out of her pocketbook and made the call.

"We lucked out. He just finished at the courthouse and was about to head back to his office. He's on his way here now. He said it will only take a few minutes."

"That's correct," said Ginny. "It's just around the corner. While we're waiting for him, Mrs. Gould, I'm going to read you your Miranda rights to save some time."

"What? Why? Does that mean you think I'm a suspect somehow?"

"Not necessarily. We do this whenever someone brings their attorney. Just to be on the safe side."

"Oh, OK. Go ahead then."

Ginny read her rights to her, and Gould acknowledged understanding them. A few minutes later, there was a knock on the door. Joe opened it and in walked Frank Driscoll.

"Hey, Joe, how've you been? Ginny."

"Hi, Frank. Didn't realize you were Mrs. Gould's lawyer."

"Small world."

Driscoll said hello to Gould and sat down next to her. "OK, Detectives, wanna bring me up to date?"

Ginny gave Driscoll a brief summary of the case, starting with Wallerman's homicide and ending with the probable murder weapon found in Gould's house just a short time ago."

"Are you sure that you found the murder weapon?"

"Not sure yet," said Joe. "The gun and two clips found with it are on their way to Ballistics as we speak. We think it'll match the bullets from the scene, but we'll have to wait and see. It's the right caliber, and it and the clips were clearly hidden."

"By my no-good son-in-law," said Gould.

"Yes, that's what we thought also," said Ginny.

"Thought?" asked Driscoll.

"Yes, we have reason to believe that the gun was hidden by Mrs. Gould."

"What! How can you—" Gould started to ask until she was cut off.

"Elizabeth, please. Don't say anything. Just listen. I'll do the talking for both of us."

"But—"

"Elizabeth!"

Then looking at Joe and then Ginny, Driscoll asked, "What made you change your thinking?"

"The facts," said Ginny.

"Can you be a little more specific?"

"Glad to," said Joe. "Mrs. Gould denied knowing anything about a gun hidden in her house. She said if there was one, it was probably hidden there by her son-in-law."

"And?"

"We got a very different story from Mrs. Gould's daughter." Joe glanced over at Gould and noticed the bead of sweat forming around her reddening forehead. "Her daughter, Adrianna, explained how she brought the gun to Mrs. Gould for her to hide so that Adrianna's husband couldn't get it. Adrianna told her mother about the incident she had with the victim, and her mother apparently was ranting and raving about what Wallerman did to her daughter."

"That's a nice story, Detective. But why should we believe Mrs. Gould's daughter? She could have been lying to protect herself. Or her husband. Or because she's afraid of her husband. Plus, you don't even know yet if the gun you found is the murder weapon."

"That's true," said Ginny. "But Ballistics will have that answer for us by tomorrow."

"Well, then let's wait and see what you learn tomorrow."

"Frank, can we talk privately?" asked Gould.

"Sure. Hold on a minute."

Joe picked up the recorder and turned it off, and he and Ginny walked out to where the chief and Porter were standing, and the chief turned off the speaker.

"I'd love to be a fly on the wall listening to their conversation," said Ginny.

"Me too. But we'll find out soon enough."

Joe called Patrol and asked them to contact Stanton and inform him that his assignment with Adrianna was now terminated, and that Ginny and he thank Stanton for his help.

Ten minutes later, Driscoll knocked on the window. Joe and Ginny walked back into the interrogation room, and Joe turned the recorder back on.

"Detectives, my client wants to make a statement. We would expect that her doing so will play a role in reducing any charges against her and any possible sentence."

Joe quickly glanced over at Ginny and could immediately tell that she was as surprised as he was.

"Frank, you know that we can't promise anything. But you've also dealt with us and the prosecutor on enough cases to know we're fair. Depending on what your client has to say, we'll do our best. In fact, Charles Porter is right outside. Why don't we have him join us?"

"Fine with us."

And with that, Porter walked in, said hello to Driscoll and introduced himself to Gould.

"Frank, what do you have for us?" asked Porter.

"That kinda depends on what you have for us."

"Fair enough. But you need to give us an inkling of what you have."

"Hypothetically speaking, if Mrs. Gould was to confess, and we're not saying she has anything to confess to, what can you do re the charges and sentencing?"

"Hypothetically answering your hypothetical question, it we received a clear confession and agreement on sentencing, we'd be willing to take murder and aggravated murder off the table. You can explain to your client that the sentences for these range from a minimum of 15 years to life without parole or even death."

"And what would you charge her with, hypothetically of course?"

"We'd be willing to go with voluntary manslaughter, giving your client the benefit of doubt that she didn't go to Wallerman's with the intent to kill him. That it was an act in the heat of the moment."

"And the recommended sentence?"

"We'd stick with the 11 years maximum."

"Any way you could see yourself lowering that?"

"Not a chance. I think my offer is one heck of a deal for your client. It won't get better. Not to mention that good behavior and early parole could basically knock that sentence in half."

"Fair enough. Give me a few minutes with my client please."

Joe turned the recorder off, but left it sitting on the table. He, Porter and Ginny left the room. They returned less than five minutes later when Driscoll knocked on the window. Joe turned the recorder back on.

"We're ready to proceed," said Driscoll. "Elizabeth, so long as you're sure I can't change your mind on this, go ahead and tell them."

"OK. Detectives, after they test the gun, they'll confirm that it is the one that killed Carl."

"Mrs. Gould," said Ginny, "how can you be so sure of that?"

"Because I'm the one who pulled the trigger. And then went home and hid the gun in the dresser."

"Mrs. Gould, why?" asked Ginny.

"Because of what that bastard did to Adrianna. He might as well have just plain raped her. He took advantage of her vulnerable situation. And used his connection to me through the town council to get close to her and get her to trust him. He deserved to die. I hope he rots in hell."

"Why did you decide to confess now?" asked Joe.

"I knew what the ballistics test would show. Plus, I realized that Adrianna would have to be a witness and talk about all that sex stuff. And you implied she might even be a suspect. She's had more than enough misery already."

"Mrs. Gould, you were alone for a while after you knew we wanted to search your house and before you spoke with your lawyer and gave us the OK. Why didn't you try to get rid of the gun?" asked Joe.

"I thought of doing that. But I was afraid you had arranged for me to be followed and I'd get caught trying to dump it someplace. Then I got the idea that if the gun was found in my house, Kenneth would be blamed for it. And that would be a nice way to get him out of Adrianna's life. So I went and wiped all the fingerprints off the gun."

"Mrs. Gould, we have your last few minutes of statement on tape," said Joe. "I'm going to get it typed up now and then ask you to sign it."

"OK. Let's just get it over with."

Joe left with the tape recorder. Twenty minutes later, he returned with three copies of five typed sheets. Gould, her lawyer and Porter read the five pages. Driscoll and Gould whispered to each other a few times, and then Gould signed all three copies.

At that point, Joe and Ginny stood up and walked right next to Gould. Ginny said, "Elizabeth Gould, you're under arrest for the voluntary manslaughter of Carl Wallerman. Please stand up and put your hands behind your back."

After a brief discussion between Gould and Driscoll, during which he said that he hoped to get Gould out on bail sometime the next day, Joe and Ginny led Gould out of the room and down the hall for fingerprinting and processing. She'd be kept in the local jail pending a likely bail hearing the next day.

Joe, Ginny and Porter spent a few minutes in the chief's office expressing relief at having Gould's confession, with the chief and Porter congratulating Joe and Ginny on their work. The case wasn't solved in the unrealistically hoped for one week, but one month for a complicated case like this was not at all bad.

And as the chief concluded, "OK, Charles. We did our part. Now we can reverse roles. We can join all the powers that be who will be pressing you to wrap this up quickly."

"Yup, fair is fair, given how I kept pushing you guys," said Porter with a smile.

Chapter 41

The next morning, Gould's bail hearing took place at 10 a.m. Driscoll did a good job of describing her as one with little risk to others or herself, and little likelihood of fleeing. Being a town council member surely didn't hurt her image. Her killing Wallerman was clearly a result of what he had done to her daughter. The prosecutor did not object, and the judge ordered that Gould could be released pending her trial on $500,000 bail.

Adrianna sat in the first row of spectators at the hearing, and had a few minutes to speak with her mother before and after the hearing. As she was leaving the courtroom, she spent a couple of minutes with Joe and Ginny.

"My God. What have I done! To my own mother!"

"Adrianna, you didn't do it," said Ginny. "All you did was tell the truth. It was your mother who did it to herself."

"But if I hadn't told you about the gun. Or if I never brought it to my mother's house. Or if I never let Wallerman get . . . "

"Don't do that to yourself," said Joe. "What happened with Wallerman, happened. And the rest, you did what you thought was right at the time. No one can do more than that."

"I know, but still," said Adrianna as she walked out of the courtroom, head hanging down and a tissue in her right hand wiping her eyes.

"I feel for her," said Ginny.

"Me too," said Joe. "But it is what it is."

By mid-afternoon, Driscoll had arranged for a bail bond, and Gould was released from jail. For the bond, Gould had to provide her equity in her house as collateral to the bail bondman and also agree to his 10 percent — $50,000 — fee. But Gould felt that was well worth her temporary freedom.

Just around lunchtime, Ballistics confirmed to Joe and Ginny that the gun that had been found in Gould's house was definitely the weapon that had killed Wallerman.

Chapter 42

Three weeks later, Joe and Ginny were sitting in the last row of seats as Gould's very brief trial got underway. The judge had both Porter and Driscoll confirm that a plea agreement had been reached and a proposed sentence agreed upon. He then had Gould and Driscoll stand, and he asked Gould a series of questions to have her publicly admit her guilt and to confirm that she understood that doing so meant giving up her rights to a jury trial, to cross-examine any witnesses and to her self-incrimination privilege. He also had her confirm that that she was pleading guilty under her own free will. Once these questions were completed, the judge addressed the sentence.

"Mrs. Gould, I hereby sentence you to 11 years in the Ohio Reformatory for Women in Marysville. Such sentence shall begin immediately. Bailiffs please remove the defendant."

And with that, Gould was handcuffed and escorted out of the courtroom by two bailiffs.

"I'm always amazed how quick it is with a confession and plea bargain," said Ginny.

"Yeah, but there's really nothing to discuss. The judge and the defendant just go through a little show to get a bunch of stuff included in the official trial transcript."

As the courtroom was emptying out of spectators,

including several reporters, Adrianna walked up to Joe and Ginny. "I wanted to say goodbye."

"Goodbye?" asked Ginny.

"Yes, I've decided that I can't stay here in Jasper Creek. Everyone now knows about Mr. Wallerman and me. And, of course, about my mother. I need a fresh start. And that means of everything. In fact, I've hired a lawyer, and we're beginning the process for me to divorce Ken."

"Wow. That's a whole lot of changes all at once. Are you sure you don't want to go a little slower to make sure these moves are right?" asked Joe.

"No, I'm sure. I'm going to move to Indianapolis."

"Indianapolis?" asked Joe.

"Yes. My aunt, my father's sister, lives there. She and her husband own a travel agency. Initially, I can live with them until I get some cash from selling my mother's house here. And they said I can work part-time at their travel agency. Oh, and I'm thinking of enrolling in college. Never too late, or so they say."

"Good for you, Adrianna," said Joe.

"And Indianapolis isn't too far away. I'll be able to visit my mother in Marysville fairly often."

"That will be nice. Well, the very best to you, Adrianna."

"Yes, definitely," said Joe.

"Thank you both. And goodbye again." And with that, Adrianna turned and walked out of the courtroom.

"Wow, Joe, talk about a few changes in your life. All at the same time."

"Yeah. I'm sure it'll be tough for her for a while. But I think she's doing the right thing. A total clean break is what she needs, including, first and foremost, getting rid of that loser of a husband. But I think she's pretty strong when she needs to be, and will come out of all this in good shape."

"And I won't even mention how excited you must be that she'll soon be unmarried and available," said Ginny with a smile.

"Yeah, but it's her loss 'cause I'm not available."

"Glad to hear that, Partner. What say we grab some lunch?"

"Works for me."

A few minutes later, Joe and Ginny were in their normal booth at Sancho's, munching on chips while waiting for their lunch.

"Boy, I really have mixed feelings on this case."

"How do you mean?" asked Joe.

"She clearly committed a crime killing Wallerman. On the other hand, given what he did to her daughter, I can understand why she did it."

"Me too. But that's understanding, not forgiving."

"I know. So in a way, the plea bargain and her relatively light sentence for a murder is probably Lady Justice stepping in and balancing the scales."

"Probably so. And let's not forget she'll probably cut her time in half with good behavior and parole."

"I know. OK, Joe, time to change the subject. We're out of excuses."

"Huh? About what?"

"About us, dummy. We've been holding off telling the chief about us until we had this case solved. It's now solved, sealed and delivered."

"You're right, Ginny," said Joe with an exaggerated gulp. "You're not gonna like this, but I'm getting cold feet."

"Joe, what's going on? We agreed to tell the chief as soon as we solved the case."

"I know. But I'm really struggling with this. I'm usually pretty decisive, maybe even a little impulsive, but not this time."

"Tell me what you're thinking."

"I feel like I was sitting on a comfortable split-rail fence. And it's changed into a sharp picket fence. And sitting on it hurts."

"Nice description, but it doesn't tell me much."

"OK, you're right. Here goes. Right now with both of us working together, loving each other and sort of living together, things are close to perfect. The only negative is our having to keep sneaking around hoping to keep our relationship secret — if it's a secret at all, which I honestly doubt. So, to me, things are, say, about 90 percent perfect."

"Agreed. No argument yet."

"If we tell the chief, and if he says 'Fine, no problem,' we jump up to 100 perfect."

"I'm still with you."

"But, if he says 'No way' and we have to stop being partners or, even worse, one of us has to leave the department, it drops down to maybe 40 or 50 percent."

"Still in agreement."

"And we have no idea which position the chief will take. Well, that seems like a lousy bet to me. We have an equal chance of things getting 10 points better or 40 or 50 points worse."

"Yikes, when you put it like that . . . but you haven't

factored in the possibility that we keep on sneaking around and then he finds out anyway. In three months or a year or three years or who knows when."

"I know. I haven't figured out how to include that in my betting analogy."

"Well, in any event, Joe, you did succeed in even further increasing my fear factor."

"Sorry about that, but you do always tell me to share my feelings with you."

"Yes I do. And I'm glad you did."

"Ah. Screw it, Ginny. Let's go talk to the chief now and get it over with."

"But, Joe …"

"I know. You can't understand me. Not to worry. I can't either. We're gonna have to tell him at some point. Sooner or later it'll leak out. We're pretty sure that half the department already knows or suspects. And we're much better off if he hears it first from us."

"Yup. I agree with that."

"And he's positive right now, what with the Wallerman case solved. We'll never be in a better position to hope-fully get the answer we want. Heck, the chief even heard Porter praising us."

"OK, Joe. I'm game if you are. But are you sure?"

"Sure's a bit too strong. But I'm about as sure as I think I'll ever be about this."

"OK, then. Let's pay and head over to the lion's den."

Chapter 43

"Chief, got a few minutes?" asked Ginny as she and Joe stood outside the chief's doorway.

"Sure. Was there a problem with the sentencing this morning?"

"No. Went just as expected. Eleven years in Marysville."

"Then why're you here? Want me to compliment you two again?"

"No, chief," said Ginny. "It's something else we need to talk to you about."

"OK. Come on in."

Joe and Ginny walked into the chief's office. Joe shut the door and he and Ginny sat down in the two visitors' chairs in front of the chief's desk.

"Closed door. This must be serious."

"It is," said Joe.

"Well, spit it out. Whatever it is."

"OK," said Ginny. "But it's not easy. This is rather personal."

"Oh?"

"Yes," said Ginny. "It's about Joe and me."

"Well, I assume it's not you two saying you're sick of working together. After Joe blew through most of the other possible partners when he first got here, you two have worked well for three or four years now."

"Yeah, it's not that," said Joe. "It's more like the opposite."

"Well, it's about damn time you came to talk to me."

"Huh?" said Joe and Ginny in unison.

"I *am* a cop, you know. And a pretty damn good one at that, if I say so myself."

"Yes, we know you are," said Ginny.

"So I hope you don't think you've been fooling me about your personal relationship."

Joe and Ginny looked at each other — Ginny watching Joe's face turn pale and Joe watching Ginny's face turn bright red.

"Chief, we weren't trying to fool you," said Ginny. "Our feelings for each other, and our personal relationship, just gradually developed over time. And then we became concerned about what the department policies, and your decision, would mean to our being able to continue as partners."

"Chief, our staying together as partners really means a lot to Ginny and me. And I think you'll agree that we're a good…"

"Hold on. Both of you. How about you give me a chance to talk?"

"Sure. Sorry, Chief," said Joe. Ginny nodded her agreement.

"First off, I'm glad you came to me. The longer that I felt that you two were sneaking, unsuccessfully I might add, behind my back, the more I'd be tempted to split you up. As punishment.

"As you probably know, we don't have a written policy to cover this. In fact, as a small department, we don't have many written policies at all. Most of what we have are just copies of stuff from the town-wide policy manual.

So that basically means I get to make the calls on most issues. And I do try to be fair. But my primary concerns are the safety and effectiveness of my employees and the department. Then comes morale within the department. And only then do I consider the individual's feelings and desires."

"Understood," said Ginny.

"OK. I'm inclined to not split you two up because your results have been so strong."

"Great! Thanks, Chief," said Ginny.

"Yes, thanks," said Joe. "What a relief."

"Hold on. There are a couple of conditions that go along with this."

"Uh oh," said Joe.

"Tell us more," added Ginny.

"You guys can remain partners as long as you don't stir up too much departmental 'talk' or otherwise negatively affect the department's morale. That means being sure not to be overly affectionate or always talking about your personal lives together in front of the others. And it's obvious that you guys are always getting coffee for each other. Try spreading that around a little. Get an occasional coffee for Jones, his desk is right near yours. Hell, bring me a coffee now and then." He paused. "Never mind, skip that, it might look too much like brown-nosing. I'll get my own coffee, but think about how easy it would be to include others in the coffee fetching. Now that I think about it, why not occasionally make it a threesome or foursome at lunch? Get my point?"

The chief looked almost avuncular as he sat behind his desk, not quite smiling, but looking more genial than they'd seen him in, well, ever. "Sure, you won't be able to chat affectionately at lunch with Jones or Caruso at your table, but you can save that for after hours. Talk shop. Maybe a threesome or a group of four of you will stir up some good ideas. You see what I'm getting at, right?

"More importantly, if your relationship or feelings for each other ever jeopardize your work, or put anyone else at increased risk, it's over. Plain and simple."

He paused, took a big breath and let it out slowly, with a look, almost, of satisfaction on his big face. "I really don't want to mess up what you two have going, not in your detective work and not in your personal lives. Believe it or not, I actually do have a heart." He grinned. Then, the stern look returned as he added, "But I want to emphasize that it's got to stay low-key, the romance stuff. Otherwise, I'll revise my decision about you two partnering. Got it?"

"Yes, Sir," said Joe while Ginny said "Yes, Chief."

"OK, then. Thanks for stopping in for this little chat. Now how about you head on back to work."

Joe and Ginny left the chief's office, both trying to hide their wide smiles as they walked back to their desks.

"Wow," said Ginny quietly once they were sitting at their desks. "That went better than we could have ever hoped for."

"Sure did."

"Now we have a whole bunch of different decisions to start thinking about. But they're all decisions with only good options."

"Very true. And I've already made the first one."

"Oh, and what might that be?"

"Garrison's," said Joe with a smile.

"Huh?"

"Tonight, my dear, we are having dinner at Garrison's. We can actually go to a restaurant right here in town."

"Right you are. Don't think we'll miss driving an hour out of town for dinner."

"Yup. And that's only the first of many great changes to occur in our lives."

"Joe, you're such a romantic."

"Maybe. Sometimes. I do know that I love you."

"Ditto right back to you. And as we make all the personal decisions we'll be facing, there's no one I'd rather be going through it all than you."

"Ditto again."

"OK. Enough of this for now. Time to get back to work."

Born in Brooklyn, NY, Stuart has lived in 7 states and 4 European countries. He and his wife now live in the foothills of the Blue Ridge Mountains. Stuart earned an engineering degree from Swarthmore College and an MBA from Harvard University. His career has included work for large multinational firms, small startups and management consulting firms. Stuart and his wife are instrument-rated private pilots and Stuart is a volunteer firefighter & EMT and a Red Cross Disaster Responder.

See what Stuart Safft is up to at his blog: https://stuartsafft.wordpress.com.

Other Books from Stuart Safft

Where's Ellen?
A Joe McFarland / Ginny Harris Mystery

Body in the Warehouse
A Joe McFarland / Ginny Harris Mystery